WAR AND PEACE

BOOK ELEVEN : 1812

By Leo Tolstoy

Double 9
BOOKS

War and Peace Book 11
by Leo Tolstoy

Copyright © 2025

ISBN: 978-93-94973-98-5

Published by

DOUBLE 9 BOOKS

2/13-B, Ansari Road
Daryaganj, New Delhi - 110002
info@double9books.com
www.double9books.com
Tel. 011-40042856

Printed in India.

About the Author

L eo Tolstoy was a Russian creator known for his books War and Peace which is viewed as the best book of pragmatist fiction. Tolstoy is additionally viewed as world's best author by quite a few people. Additionally an ethical scholar and a social reformer, Tolstoy had extreme moralistic points of view. In later life, he turned into an intense Christian rebel and anarcho-conservative.

Leo Tolstoy Born in Yasnaya Polyana on September 9, 1828, He had a place with a notable honorable Russian family. He was the fourth among five offspring of Count Nikolai Ilyich Tolstoy and Countess Mariya Tolstaya, both of whom kicked the bucket passing on their youngsters to be raised by family members.

In 1844, Tolstoy was acknowledged into Kazan University. Incapable to graduate past the subsequent year, Tolstoy got back to Yasnava Polyana and afterward invested energy going among Moscow and St. Petersburg. With some functioning information on a few dialects, he turned into a multilingual. Yet again the recently observed youth pulled in Tolstoy towards drinking, visiting massage parlors and most betting which left him in weighty obligation and anguish however Tolstoy before long acknowledged he was carrying on with a brutish life and endeavored college tests with the expectation that he would acquire a situation with the public authority, yet finished yet up in Caucuses serving in the military continuing in the strides of his senior sibling.

In Year 1862, Leo Tolstoy wedded Sophia Andreevna Behrs, generally called Sonya, who was 16 years more youthful than him. The couple had thirteen youngsters, of which, five passed on at an early age. Sonya went about as Tolstoy's secretary, editor and monetary chief while he made two out of his most prominent works. Their initial wedded life was loaded up with happiness.

He started composing his show-stopper, War and Peace in 1862. The six volumes of the work were distributed somewhere in the range of 1863 and 1869. With 580 characters got from history and others made by Tolstoy, this extraordinary novel takes on investigating the hypothesis of history and the irrelevance of noted figures like Alexander and Napoleon. Anna Karenina, Tolstoy's next epic was begun in 1873 and distributed totally in 1878.

Contents

BOOK ELEVEN : 1812

CHAPTER I

A bsolute continuity of motion is not comprehensible to the human mind. Laws of motion of any kind become comprehensible to man only when he examines arbitrarily selected elements of that motion; but at the same time, a large proportion of human error comes from the arbitrary division of continuous motion into discontinuous elements. There is a well-known, so-called sophism of the ancients consisting in this, that Achilles could never catch up with a tortoise he was following, in spite of the fact that he traveled ten times as fast as the tortoise. By the time Achilles has covered the distance that separated him from the tortoise, the tortoise has covered one tenth of that distance ahead of him: when Achilles has covered that tenth, the tortoise has covered another one hundredth, and so on forever. This problem seemed to the ancients insoluble. The absurd answer (that Achilles could never overtake the tortoise) resulted from this: that motion was arbitrarily divided into discontinuous elements, whereas the motion both of Achilles and of the tortoise was continuous.

By adopting smaller and smaller elements of motion we only approach a solution of the problem, but never reach it. Only when we have admitted the conception of the infinitely small, and the resulting geometrical progression with a common ratio of one tenth, and have found the sum of this progression to infinity, do we reach a solution of the problem.

A modern branch of mathematics having achieved the art of dealing with the infinitely small can now yield solutions in other more complex problems of motion which used to appear insoluble.

This modern branch of mathematics, unknown to the ancients, when dealing with problems of motion admits the conception of the infinitely small, and so conforms to the chief condition of motion (absolute continuity) and thereby corrects the inevitable error which the human mind cannot avoid when it deals with separate elements of motion instead of examining continuous motion.

In seeking the laws of historical movement just the same thing happens. The movement of humanity, arising as it does from innumerable arbitrary human wills, is continuous.

To understand the laws of this continuous movement is the aim of history. But to arrive at these laws, resulting from the sum of all those human wills, man's mind postulates arbitrary and disconnected units. The first method of history is to take an arbitrarily selected series of continuous events and examine it apart from others, though there is and can be no *beginning* to any event, for one event always flows uninterruptedly from another.

The second method is to consider the actions of some one man—a king or a commander—as equivalent to the sum of many individual wills; whereas the sum of individual wills is never expressed by the activity of a single historic personage.

Historical science in its endeavor to draw nearer to truth continually takes smaller and smaller units for examination. But however small the units it takes, we feel that to take any unit disconnected from others, or to assume a *beginning* of any phenomenon, or to say that the will of many men is expressed by the actions of any one historic personage, is in itself false.

It needs no critical exertion to reduce utterly to dust any deductions drawn from history. It is merely necessary to select some larger or smaller unit as the subject of observation—as criticism has every right to do, seeing that whatever unit history observes must always be arbitrarily selected.

Only by taking infinitesimally small units for observation (the differential of history, that is, the individual tendencies of men) and attaining to the art of integrating them (that is, finding the sum of these infinitesimals) can we hope to arrive at the laws of history.

The first fifteen years of the nineteenth century in Europe present an extraordinary movement of millions of people. Men leave their customary pursuits, hasten from one side of Europe to the other, plunder and slaughter one another, triumph and are plunged in despair, and for some years the whole course of life is altered and presents an intensive movement which first increases and then slackens. What was the cause of this movement, by what laws was it governed? asks the mind of man.

The historians, replying to this question, lay before us the sayings and doings of a few dozen men in a building in the city of Paris, calling these sayings and doings "the Revolution"; then they give a detailed biography of Napoleon and of certain people favorable or hostile to him; tell of the influence some of these people had on others, and say: that is why this movement took place and those are its laws.

But the mind of man not only refuses to believe this explanation, but plainly says that this method of explanation is fallacious, because in it a weaker phenomenon is taken as the cause of a stronger. The sum of human wills produced the Revolution and Napoleon, and only the sum of those wills first tolerated and then destroyed them.

"But every time there have been conquests there have been conquerors; every time there has been a revolution in any state there have been great men," says history. And, indeed, human reason replies: every time conquerors appear there have been wars, but this does not prove that the conquerors caused the wars and that it is possible to find the laws of a war in the personal activity of a single man. Whenever I look at my watch and its hands point to ten, I hear the bells of the neighboring church; but because the bells begin to ring when the hands of the clock reach ten, I have no right to assume that the movement of the bells is caused by the position of the hands of the watch.

Whenever I see the movement of a locomotive I hear the whistle and see the valves opening and wheels turning; but I have no right to conclude that the whistling and the turning of wheels are the cause of the movement of the engine.

The peasants say that a cold wind blows in late spring because the oaks are budding, and really every spring cold winds do blow when the oak is budding. But though I do not know what causes the cold winds to blow when the oak buds unfold, I cannot agree with the peasants that the unfolding of the oak buds is the cause of the cold wind, for the force of the wind is beyond the influence of the buds. I see only a coincidence of occurrences such as happens with all the phenomena of life, and I see that however much and however carefully I observe the hands of the watch, and the valves and wheels of the engine, and the oak, I shall not discover the cause of the bells ringing, the engine moving, or of the winds of spring. To that I must entirely change my point of view and study the laws of the movement of steam, of the bells, and of the wind. History must do the same. And attempts in this direction have already been made.

To study the laws of history we must completely change the subject of our observation, must leave aside kings, ministers, and generals, and study the common, infinitesimally small elements by which the masses are moved. No one can say in how far it is possible for man to advance in this way toward an understanding of the laws of history; but it is evident that only along that path does the possibility of discovering the laws of history lie, and that as yet not a millionth part as much mental effort has been applied in this direction by historians as has been devoted to describing the actions of various kings, commanders, and ministers and propounding the historians' own reflections concerning these actions.

CHAPTER II

The forces of a dozen European nations burst into Russia. The Russian army and people avoided a collision till Smolénsk was reached, and again from Smolénsk to Borodinó. The French army pushed on to Moscow, its goal, its impetus ever increasing as it neared its aim, just as the velocity of a falling body increases as it approaches the earth. Behind it were seven hundred miles of hunger-stricken, hostile country; ahead were a few dozen miles separating it from its goal. Every soldier in Napoleon's army felt this and the invasion moved on by its own momentum.

The more the Russian army retreated the more fiercely a spirit of hatred of the enemy flared up, and while it retreated the army increased and consolidated. At Borodinó a collision took place. Neither army was broken up, but the Russian army retreated immediately after the collision as inevitably as a ball recoils after colliding with another having a greater momentum, and with equal inevitability the ball of invasion that had advanced with such momentum rolled on for some distance, though the collision had deprived it of all its force.

The Russians retreated eighty miles—to beyond Moscow—and the French reached Moscow and there came to a standstill. For five weeks after that there was not a single battle. The French did not move. As a bleeding, mortally wounded animal licks its wounds, they remained inert in Moscow for five weeks, and then suddenly, with no fresh reason, fled back: they made a dash for the Kalúga road, and (after a victory—for at Málo-Yaroslávets the field of conflict again remained theirs) without undertaking a single serious battle, they fled still more rapidly back to Smolénsk, beyond Smolénsk, beyond the Berëzina, beyond Vílna, and farther still.

On the evening of the twenty-sixth of August, Kutúzov and the whole Russian army were convinced that the battle of Borodinó was a victory. Kutúzov reported so to the Emperor. He gave orders to prepare for a fresh conflict to finish the enemy and did this not to deceive anyone, but because he knew that the enemy was beaten, as everyone who had taken part in the battle knew it.

But all that evening and next day reports came in one after another of unheard-of losses, of the loss of half the army, and a fresh battle proved physically impossible.

It was impossible to give battle before information had been collected, the wounded gathered in, the supplies of ammunition replenished, the slain reckoned up, new officers appointed to replace those who had been killed, and before the men had had food and sleep. And meanwhile, the very next morning after the battle, the French army advanced of itself upon the Russians, carried forward by the force of its own momentum now seemingly increased in inverse proportion to the square of the distance from its aim. Kutúzov's wish was to attack next day, and the whole army desired to do so. But to make an attack the wish to do so is not sufficient, there must also be a possibility of doing it, and that possibility did not exist. It was impossible not to retreat a day's march, and then in the same way it was impossible not to retreat another and a third day's march, and at last, on the first of September when the army drew near Moscow—despite the strength of the feeling that had arisen in all ranks—the force of circumstances compelled it to retire beyond Moscow. And the troops retired one more, last, day's march, and abandoned Moscow to the enemy.

For people accustomed to think that plans of campaign and battles are made by generals—as anyone of us sitting over a map in his study may imagine how he would have arranged things in this or that battle—the questions present themselves: Why did Kutúzov during the retreat not do this or that? Why did he not take up a position before reaching Filí? Why did he not retire at once by the Kalúga road, abandoning Moscow? and so on. People accustomed to think in that way forget, or do not know, the inevitable conditions which always limit the activities of any commander in chief. The activity of a commander in chief does not at all resemble the activity we imagine to ourselves when we sit at ease in our studies examining some campaign on the map, with a certain number of troops on this and that side in a certain known locality, and begin our plans from some given moment. A commander in chief is never dealing with the *beginning* of any event—the position from which we always contemplate it. The commander in chief is always in the midst of a series of shifting events and so he never can at any moment consider the whole import of an event that is occurring. Moment by moment the event is imperceptibly shaping itself, and at every moment of this continuous, uninterrupted shaping of events the commander in chief is in the midst of a most complex play of intrigues, worries, contingencies, authorities, projects, counsels, threats, and deceptions and is continually obliged to reply to innumerable questions addressed to him, which constantly conflict with one another.

Learned military authorities quite seriously tell us that Kutúzov should have moved his army to the Kalúga road long before reaching Filí, and that somebody actually submitted such a proposal to him. But a commander in chief, especially at a difficult moment, has always before him not one proposal but dozens simultaneously. And all these proposals, based on strategics and tactics, contradict each other.

A commander in chief's business, it would seem, is simply to choose one of these projects. But even that he cannot do. Events and time do not wait. For instance, on the twenty-eighth it is suggested to him to cross to the Kalúga road, but just then an adjutant gallops up from Milorádovich asking whether he is to engage the French or retire. An order must be given him at once, that instant. And the order to retreat carries us past the turn to the Kalúga road. And after the adjutant comes the commissary general asking where the stores are to be taken, and the chief of the hospitals asks where the wounded are to go, and a courier from Petersburg brings a letter from the sovereign which does not admit of the possibility of abandoning Moscow, and the commander in chief's rival, the man who is undermining him (and there are always not merely one but several such), presents a new project diametrically opposed to that of turning to the Kalúga road, and the commander in chief himself needs sleep and refreshment to maintain his energy and a respectable general who has been overlooked in the distribution of rewards comes to complain, and the inhabitants of the district pray to be defended, and an officer sent to inspect the locality comes in and gives a report quite contrary to what was said by the officer previously sent; and a spy, a prisoner, and a general who has been on reconnaissance, all describe the position of the enemy's army differently. People accustomed to misunderstand or to forget these inevitable conditions of a commander in chief's actions describe to us, for instance, the position of the army at Filí and assume that the commander in chief could, on the first of September, quite freely decide whether to abandon Moscow or defend it; whereas, with the Russian army less than four miles from Moscow, no such question existed. When had that question been settled? At Drissa and at Smolénsk and most palpably of all on the twenty-fourth of August at Shevárdino and on the twenty-sixth at Borodinó, and each day and hour and minute of the retreat from Borodinó to Filí.

CHAPTER III

When Ermólov, having been sent by Kutúzov to inspect the position, told the field marshal that it was impossible to fight there before Moscow and that they must retreat, Kutúzov looked at him in silence.

"Give me your hand," said he and, turning it over so as to feel the pulse, added: "You are not well, my dear fellow. Think what you are saying!"

Kutúzov could not yet admit the possibility of retreating beyond Moscow without a battle.

On the Poklónny Hill, four miles from the Dorogomílov gate of Moscow, Kutúzov got out of his carriage and sat down on a bench by the roadside. A great crowd of generals gathered round him, and Count Rostopchín, who had come out from Moscow, joined them. This brilliant company separated into several groups who all discussed the advantages and disadvantages of the position, the state of the army, the plans suggested, the situation of Moscow, and military questions generally. Though they had not been summoned for the purpose, and though it was not so called, they all felt that this was really a council of war. The conversations all dealt with public questions. If anyone gave or asked for personal news, it was done in a whisper and they immediately reverted to general matters. No jokes, or laughter, or smiles even, were seen among all these men. They evidently all made an effort to hold themselves at the height the situation demanded. And all these groups, while talking among themselves, tried to keep near the commander in chief (whose bench formed the center of the gathering) and to speak so that he might overhear them. The commander in chief listened to what was being said and sometimes asked them to repeat their remarks, but did not himself take part in the conversations or express any opinion. After hearing what was being said by one or other of these groups he generally turned away with an air of disappointment, as though they were not speaking of anything he wished to hear. Some discussed the position that had been chosen, criticizing not the position itself so much as the mental capacity of those who had chosen it. Others argued that a mistake had been made earlier and that a battle should have been fought two days before. Others again spoke of the battle of Salamanca, which was described by Crosart, a newly arrived Frenchman in a Spanish uniform. (This Frenchman and one of the German princes serving with the Russian army were discussing the siege of Saragossa and considering the possibility of defending Moscow in a similar manner.) Count Rostopchín was telling a fourth group that he was prepared to die with the city train bands under the walls of the capital, but that he still could not help regretting having been left in ignorance of what was happening, and that had he known it sooner things would have been different.... A fifth group, displaying the profundity of their strategic perceptions, discussed the direction the troops would now have to take. A sixth group was talking absolute nonsense. Kutúzov's expression grew more and more preoccupied and gloomy. From all this talk he saw only one thing: that to defend Moscow was a *physical impossibility* in the full meaning of those words, that is to say, so utterly impossible that if any senseless commander were to give orders to fight, confusion would result but the battle would still not take place. It would not take place because the commanders not merely all recognized the position to be impossible, but in their conversations were only discussing what would happen after its inevitable abandonment. How could the commanders lead their troops to a field of battle they considered impossible to hold? The lower-grade officers and even the soldiers (who too reason) also considered the position impossible and therefore could not go to fight, fully convinced as they were of defeat. If Bennigsen insisted on the position being defended and others still discussed it, the question was no longer important in itself but only as a pretext for disputes and intrigue. This Kutúzov knew well.

Bennigsen, who had chosen the position, warmly displayed his Russian patriotism (Kutúzov could not listen to this without wincing) by insisting that Moscow must be defended. His aim was as clear as daylight to Kutúzov: if the defense failed, to throw the blame on Kutúzov who had brought the army as far as the Sparrow Hills without giving battle; if it succeeded, to claim the success as his own; or if battle were not given, to clear himself of the crime of abandoning Moscow. But this intrigue did not now occupy the old man's mind. One terrible question absorbed him and to that question he heard no reply from anyone. The question for him now was: "Have I really allowed Napoleon to reach Moscow, and when did I do so? When was it decided? Can it have been yesterday when I ordered Plátov to retreat, or was it the evening before, when I had a nap and told Bennigsen to issue orders? Or was it earlier still?... When, when was this terrible affair decided? Moscow must be abandoned. The army must retreat and the order to do so must be given." To give that terrible order seemed to him equivalent to resigning the command of the army. And not only did he love power to which he was accustomed (the honours awarded to Prince Prozoróvski, under whom he had served in Turkey, galled him), but he was convinced that he was destined to save Russia and that that was why, against the Emperor's wish and by the will of the people, he had been chosen commander in chief. He was convinced that he alone could maintain command of the army in these difficult circumstances, and that in all the world he alone could encounter the invincible Napoleon without fear, and he was horrified at the thought of the order he had to issue. But something had to be decided, and these conversations around him which were assuming too free a character must be stopped.

He called the most important generals to him.

"My head, be it good or bad, must depend on itself," said he, rising from the bench, and he rode to Filí where his carriages were waiting.

CHAPTER IV

The Council of War began to assemble at two in the afternoon in the better and roomier part of Andrew Savostyánov's hut. The men, women, and children of the large peasant family crowded into the back room across the passage. Only Malásha, Andrew's six-year-old granddaughter whom his Serene Highness had petted and to whom he had given a lump of sugar while drinking his tea, remained on the top of the brick oven in the larger room. Malásha looked down from the oven with shy delight at the faces, uniforms, and decorations of the generals, who one after another came into the room and sat down on the broad benches in the corner under the icons. "Granddad" himself, as Malásha in her own mind called Kutúzov, sat apart in a dark corner behind the oven. He sat, sunk deep in a folding armchair, and continually cleared his throat and pulled at the collar of his coat which, though it was unbuttoned, still seemed to pinch his neck. Those who entered went up one by one to the field marshal; he pressed the hands of some and nodded to others. His adjutant Kaysárov was about to draw back the curtain of the window facing Kutúzov, but the latter moved his hand angrily and Kaysárovunderstood that his Serene Highness did not wish his face to be seen.

Round the peasant's deal table, on which lay maps, plans, pencils, and papers, so many people gathered that the orderlies brought in another bench and put it beside the table. Ermólov, Kaysárov, and Toll, who had just arrived, sat down on this bench. In the foremost place, immediately under the icons, sat Barclay de Tolly, his high forehead merging into his bald crown. He had a St. George's Cross round his neck and looked pale and ill. He had been feverish for two days and was now shivering and in pain. Beside him sat Uvárov, who with rapid gesticulations was giving him some information, speaking in low tones as they all did. Chubby little Dokhtúrov was listening attentively with eyebrows raised and arms folded on his stomach. On the other side sat Count Ostermann-Tolstóy, seemingly absorbed in his own thoughts. His broad head with its bold features and glittering eyes was resting on his hand. Raévski, twitching forward the black hair on his temples as was his habit, glanced now at Kutúzov and now at the door with a look of impatience. Konovnítsyn's firm, handsome, and kindly face was lit up by a tender, sly smile. His glance met Malásha's, and the expression of his eyes caused the little girl to smile.

They were all waiting for Bennigsen, who on the pretext of inspecting the position was finishing his savory dinner. They waited for him from four till six o'clock and did not begin their deliberations all that time but talked in low tones of other matters.

Only when Bennigsen had entered the hut did Kutúzov leave his corner and draw toward the table, but not near enough for the candles that had been placed there to light up his face.

Bennigsen opened the council with the question: "Are we to abandon Russia's ancient and sacred capital without a struggle, or are we to defend it?" A prolonged and general silence followed. There was a frown on every face and only Kutúzov's angry grunts and occasional cough broke the silence. All eyes were gazing at him. Malásha too looked at "Granddad." She was nearest to him and saw how his face puckered; he seemed about to cry, but this did not last long.

"Russia's ancient and sacred capital!" he suddenly said, repeating Bennigsen's words in an angry voice and thereby drawing attention to the false note in them. "Allow me to tell you, your excellency, that that question has no meaning for a Russian." (He lurched his heavy body forward.) "Such a question cannot be put; it is senseless! The question I have asked these gentlemen to meet to discuss is a military one. The question is that of saving Russia. Is it better to give up Moscow without a battle, or by accepting battle to risk losing the army as well as Moscow? That is the question on which I want your opinion," and he sank back in his chair.

The discussion began. Bennigsen did not yet consider his game lost. Admitting the view of Barclay and others that a defensive battle at Filí was impossible, but imbued with Russian patriotism and the love of Moscow, he proposed to move troops from the right to the left flank during the night and attack the French right flank the following day. Opinions were divided, and arguments were advanced for and against that project. Ermólov, Dokhtúrov, and Raévski agreed with Bennigsen. Whether feeling it necessary to make a sacrifice before abandoning the capital or guided by other, personal considerations, these generals seemed not to understand that this council could not alter the inevitable course of events and that Moscow was in effect already abandoned. The other generals, however, understood it and, leaving aside the question of Moscow, spoke of the direction the army should take in its retreat. Malásha, who kept her eyes fixed on what was going on before her, understood the meaning of the council differently. It seemed to her that it was only a personal struggle between "Granddad" and "Long-coat" as she termed Bennigsen. She saw that they grew spiteful when they spoke to one another, and in her heart she sided with "Granddad." In the midst of the conversation she noticed "Granddad" give Bennigsen a quick, subtle glance, and then to her joys she saw that "Granddad" said something to "Long-coat" which settled him. Bennigsen suddenly reddened and paced angrily up and down the room. What so affected him was Kutúzov's calm and quiet comment on the advantage or disadvantage of Bennigsen's proposal to move troops by night from the right to the left flank to attack the French right wing.

"Gentlemen," said Kutúzov, "I cannot approve of the count's plan. Moving troops in close proximity to an enemy is always dangerous, and military history supports that view. For instance..." Kutúzov seemed to reflect, searching for an example, then with a clear, naïve look at Bennigsen he added: "Oh yes; take the battle of Friedland, which I think the count well remembers, and which was... not fully successful, only because our troops were rearranged too near the enemy...."

There followed a momentary pause, which seemed very long to them all.

The discussion recommenced, but pauses frequently occurred and they all felt that there was no more to be said.

During one of these pauses Kutúzov heaved a deep sigh as if preparing to speak. They all looked at him.

"Well, gentlemen, I see that it is I who will have to pay for the broken crockery," said he, and rising slowly he moved to the table. "Gentlemen, I have heard your views. Some of you will not agree with me. But I," he paused, "by the authority entrusted to me by my Sovereign and country, order a retreat."

After that the generals began to disperse with the solemnity and circumspect silence of people who are leaving, after a funeral.

Some of the generals, in low tones and in a strain very different from the way they had spoken during the council, communicated something to their commander in chief.

Malásha, who had long been expected for supper, climbed carefully backwards down from the oven, her bare little feet catching at its projections, and slipping between the legs of the generals she darted out of the room.

When he had dismissed the generals Kutúzov sat a long time with his elbows on the table, thinking always of the same terrible question: "When, when did the abandonment of Moscow become inevitable? When was that done which settled the matter? And who was to blame for it?"

"I did not expect this," said he to his adjutant Schneider when the latter came in late that night. "I did not expect this! I did not think this would happen."

"You should take some rest, your Serene Highness," replied Schneider.

"But no! They shall eat horseflesh yet, like the Turks!" exclaimed Kutúzov without replying, striking the table with his podgy fist. "They shall too, if only..."

CHAPTER V

At that very time, in circumstances even more important than retreating without a battle, namely the evacuation and burning of Moscow, Rostopchín, who is usually represented as being the instigator of that event, acted in an altogether different manner from Kutúzov.

After the battle of Borodinó the abandonment and burning of Moscow was as inevitable as the retreat of the army beyond Moscow without fighting.

Every Russian might have predicted it, not by reasoning but by the feeling implanted in each of us and in our fathers.

The same thing that took place in Moscow had happened in all the towns and villages on Russian soil beginning with Smolénsk, without the participation of Count Rostopchín and his broadsheets. The people awaited the enemy unconcernedly, did not riot or become excited or tear anyone to pieces, but faced its fate, feeling within it the strength to find what it should do at that most difficult moment. And as soon as the enemy drew near the wealthy classes went away abandoning their property, while the poorer remained and burned and destroyed what was left.

The consciousness that this would be so and would always be so was and is present in the heart of every Russian. And a consciousness of this, and a foreboding that Moscow would be taken, was present in Russian Moscow society in 1812. Those who had quitted Moscow already in July and at the beginning of August showed that they expected this. Those who went away, taking what they could and abandoning their houses and half their belongings, did so from the latent patriotism which expresses itself not by phrases or by giving one's children to save the fatherland and similar unnatural exploits, but unobtrusively, simply, organically, and therefore in the way that always produces the most powerful results.

"It is disgraceful to run away from danger; only cowards are running away from Moscow," they were told. In his broadsheets Rostopchín impressed on them that to leave Moscow was shameful. They were ashamed to be called cowards, ashamed to leave, but still they left, knowing it had to be done. Why did they go? It is impossible to suppose that Rostopchín had scared them by his accounts of horrors Napoleon had committed in conquered countries. The first people to go away were the rich educated people who knew quite well that Vienna and Berlin had remained intact and that during Napoleon's occupation the inhabitants had spent their time pleasantly in the company of the charming Frenchmen whom the Russians, and especially the Russian ladies, then liked so much.

They went away because for Russians there could be no question as to whether things would go well or ill under French rule in Moscow. It was out of the question to be under French rule, it would be the worst thing that could happen. They went away even before the battle of Borodinó and still more rapidly after it, despite Rostopchín's calls to defend Moscow or the announcement of his intention to take the wonder-working icon of the Iberian Mother of God and go to fight, or of the balloons that were to destroy the French, and despite all the nonsense Rostopchín wrote in his broadsheets. They knew that it was for the army to fight, and that if it could not succeed it would not do to take young ladies and house serfs to the Three Hills quarter of Moscow to fight Napoleon, and that they must go away, sorry as they were to abandon their property to destruction. They went away without thinking of the tremendous significance of that immense and wealthy city being given over to destruction, for a great city with wooden buildings was certain when abandoned by its inhabitants to be burned. They went away each on his own account, and yet it was only in consequence of their going away that the momentous event was accomplished that will always remain the greatest glory of the Russian people. The lady who, afraid of being stopped by Count Rostopchín's orders, had already in June moved with her Negroes and her women jesters from Moscow to her Sarátov estate, with a vague consciousness that she was not Bonaparte's servant, was really, simply, and truly carrying out the great work which saved Russia. But Count Rostopchín, who now taunted those who left Moscow and now had the government offices removed; now distributed quite useless weapons to the drunken rabble; now had processions displaying the icons, and now forbade Father Augustin to remove icons or the relics of saints; now seized all the private carts in Moscow and on one hundred and thirty-six of them removed the balloon that was being constructed by Leppich; now hinted that he would burn Moscow and related how he had set fire to his own house; now wrote a proclamation to the French solemnly upbraiding them for having destroyed his Orphanage; now claimed the glory of having hinted that he would burn Moscow and now repudiated the deed; now ordered the people to catch all spies and bring them to him, and now reproached them for doing so; now expelled all the French residents from Moscow, and now allowed Madame Aubert-Chalmé (the center of the whole French colony in Moscow) to remain, but ordered the venerable old postmaster Klyucharëv to be arrested and exiled for no particular offense; now assembled the people at the Three Hills to fight the French and now, to get rid of them, handed over to them a man to be killed and himself drove away by a back gate; now declared that he would not survive the fall of Moscow, and now wrote French verses in albums concerning his share in the affair—this man did not understand the meaning of what was happening but merely wanted to do something himself that would astonish people, to perform some patriotically heroic feat; and like a child he made sport of the momentous, and unavoidable event—the abandonment and burning of Moscow—and tried with his puny hand now to speed and now to stay the enormous, popular tide that bore him along with it.

CHAPTER VI

H élène, having returned with the court from Vílna to Petersburg, found herself in a difficult position.

In Petersburg she had enjoyed the special protection of a grandee who occupied one of the highest posts in the Empire. In Vílna she had formed an intimacy with a young foreign prince. When she returned to Petersburg both the magnate and the prince were there, and both claimed their rights. Hélène was faced by a new problem—how to preserve her intimacy with both without offending either.

What would have seemed difficult or even impossible to another woman did not cause the least embarrassment to Countess Bezúkhova, who evidently deserved her reputation of being a very clever woman. Had she attempted concealment, or tried to extricate herself from her awkward position by cunning, she would have spoiled her case by acknowledging herself guilty. But Hélène, like a really great man who can do whatever he pleases, at once assumed her own position to be correct, as she sincerely believed it to be, and that everyone else was to blame.

The first time the young foreigner allowed himself to reproach her, she lifted her beautiful head and, half turning to him, said firmly: "That's just like a man—selfish and cruel! I expected nothing else. A woman sacrifices herself for you, she suffers, and this is her reward! What right have you, monseigneur, to demand an account of my attachments and friendships? He is a man who has been more than a father to me!" The prince was about to say something, but Hélène interrupted him.

"Well, yes," said she, "it may be that he has other sentiments for me than those of a father, but that is not a reason for me to shut my door on him. I am not a man, that I should repay kindness with ingratitude! Know, monseigneur, that in all that relates to my intimate feelings I render account only to God and to my conscience," she concluded, laying her hand on her beautiful, fully expanded bosom and looking up to heaven.

"But for heaven's sake listen to me!"

"Marry me, and I will be your slave!"

"But that's impossible."

"You won't deign to demean yourself by marrying me, you..." said Hélène, beginning to cry.

The prince tried to comfort her, but Hélène, as if quite distraught, said through her tears that there was nothing to prevent her marrying, that there were precedents (there were up to that time very few, but she mentioned Napoleon and some other exalted personages), that she had never been her husband's wife, and that she had been sacrificed.

"But the law, religion..." said the prince, already yielding.

"The law, religion... What have they been invented for if they can't arrange that?" said Hélène.

The prince was surprised that so simple an idea had not occurred to him, and he applied for advice to the holy brethren of the Society of Jesus, with whom he was on intimate terms.

A few days later at one of those enchanting fetes which Hélène gave at her country house on the Stone Island, the charming Monsieur de Jobert, a man no longer young, with snow white hair and brilliant black eyes, a Jesuit *à robe courte* * was presented to her, and in the garden by the light of the illuminations and to the sound of music talked to her for a long time of the love of God, of Christ, of the Sacred Heart, and of the consolations the one true Catholic religion affords in this world and the next. Hélène was touched, and more than once tears rose to her eyes and to those of Monsieur de Jobert and their voices trembled. A dance, for which her partner came to seek her, put an end to her discourse with her future *directeur de conscience*, but the next evening Monsieur de Jobert came to see Hélène when she was alone, and after that often came again.

* Lay member of the Society of Jesus.

One day he took the countess to a Roman Catholic church, where she knelt down before the altar to which she was led. The enchanting, middle-aged Frenchman laid his hands on her head and, as she herself afterward described it, she felt something like a fresh breeze wafted into her soul. It was explained to her that this was *la grâce*.

After that a long-frocked abbé was brought to her. She confessed to him, and he absolved her from her sins. Next day she received a box containing the Sacred Host, which was left at her house for her to partake of. A few days later Hélène learned with pleasure that she had now been admitted to the true Catholic Church and that in a few days the Pope himself would hear of her and would send her a certain document.

All that was done around her and to her at this time, all the attention devoted to her by so many clever men and expressed in such pleasant, refined ways, and the state of dove-like purity she was now in (she wore only white dresses and white ribbons all that time) gave her pleasure, but her pleasure did not cause her for a moment to forget her aim. And as it always happens in contests of cunning that a stupid person gets the better of cleverer ones, Hélène—having realized that the main object of all these words and all this trouble was, after converting her to Catholicism, to obtain money from her for Jesuit institutions (as to which she received indications)—before parting with her money insisted that the various operations necessary to free her from her husband should be performed. In her view the aim of every religion was merely to preserve certain proprieties while affording satisfaction to human desires. And with this aim, in one of her talks with her Father Confessor, she insisted on an answer to the question, in how far was she bound by her marriage?

They were sitting in the twilight by a window in the drawing room. The scent of flowers came in at the window. Hélène was wearing a white dress, transparent over her shoulders and bosom. The abbé, a well-fed man with a plump, clean-shaven chin, a pleasant firm mouth, and white hands meekly folded on his knees, sat close to Hélène and, with a subtle smile on his lips and a peaceful look of delight at her beauty, occasionally glanced at her face as he explained his opinion on the subject. Hélène with an uneasy smile looked at his curly hair and his plump, clean-shaven, blackish cheeks and every moment expected the conversation to take a fresh turn. But the abbé, though he evidently enjoyed the beauty of his companion, was absorbed in his mastery of the matter.

The course of the Father Confessor's arguments ran as follows: "Ignorant of the import of what you were undertaking, you made a vow of conjugal fidelity to a man who on his part, by entering the married state without faith in the religious significance of marriage, committed an act of sacrilege. That marriage lacked the dual significance it should have had. Yet in spite of this your vow was binding. You swerved from it. What did you commit by so acting? A venial, or a mortal, sin? A venial sin, for you acted without evil intention. If now you married again with the object of bearing children, your sin might be forgiven. But the question is again a twofold one: firstly..."

But suddenly Hélène, who was getting bored, said with one of her bewitching smiles: "But I think that having espoused the true religion I cannot be bound by what a false religion laid upon me."

The director of her conscience was astounded at having the case presented to him thus with the simplicity of Columbus' egg. He was delighted at the unexpected rapidity of his pupil's progress, but could not abandon the edifice of argument he had laboriously constructed.

"Let us understand one another, Countess," said he with a smile, and began refuting his spiritual daughter's arguments.

CHAPTER VII

Hélène understood that the question was very simple and easy from the ecclesiastical point of view, and that her directors were making difficulties only because they were apprehensive as to how the matter would be regarded by the secular authorities.

So she decided that it was necessary to prepare the opinion of society. She provoked the jealousy of the elderly magnate and told him what she had told her other suitor; that is, she put the matter so that the only way for him to obtain a right over her was to marry her. The elderly magnate was at first as much taken aback by this suggestion of marriage with a woman whose husband was alive, as the younger man had been, but Hélène's imperturbable conviction that it was as simple and natural as marrying a maiden had its effect on him too. Had Hélène herself shown the least sign of hesitation, shame, or secrecy, her cause would certainly have been lost; but not only did she show no signs of secrecy or shame, on the contrary, with good-natured naïveté she told her intimate friends (and these were all Petersburg) that both the prince and the magnate had proposed to her and that she loved both and was afraid of grieving either.

A rumor immediately spread in Petersburg, not that Hélène wanted to be divorced from her husband (had such a report spread many would have opposed so illegal an intention) but simply that the unfortunate and interesting Hélène was in doubt which of the two men she should marry. The question was no longer whether this was possible, but only which was the better match and how the matter would be regarded at court. There were, it is true, some rigid individuals unable to rise to the height of such a question, who saw in the project a desecration of the sacrament of marriage, but there were not many such and they remained silent, while the majority were interested in Hélène's good fortune and in the question which match would be the more advantageous. Whether it was right or wrong to remarry while one had a husband living they did not discuss, for that question had evidently been settled by people "wiser than you or me," as they said, and to doubt the correctness of that decision would be to risk exposing one's stupidity and incapacity to live in society.

Only MáryaDmítrievnaAkhrosímova, who had come to Petersburg that summer to see one of her sons, allowed herself plainly to express an opinion contrary to the general one. Meeting Hélène at a ball she stopped her in the middle of the room and, amid general silence, said in her gruff voice: "So wives of living men have started marrying again! Perhaps you think you have invented a novelty? You have been forestalled, my dear! It was thought of long ago. It is done in all the brothels," and with these words MáryaDmítrievna, turning up her wide sleeves with her usual threatening gesture and glancing sternly round, moved across the room.

Though people were afraid of MáryaDmítrievna she was regarded in Petersburg as a buffoon, and so of what she had said they only noticed, and repeated in a whisper, the one coarse word she had used, supposing the whole sting of her remark to lie in that word.

Prince Vasíli, who of late very often forgot what he had said and repeated one and the same thing a hundred times, remarked to his daughter whenever he chanced to see her:

"Hélène, I have a word to say to you," and he would lead her aside, drawing her hand downward. "I have heard of certain projects concerning... you know. Well my dear child, you know how your father's heart rejoices to know that you... You have suffered so much.... But, my dear child, consult only your own heart. That is all I have to say," and concealing his unvarying emotion he would press his cheek against his daughter's and move away.

Bilíbin, who had not lost his reputation of an exceedingly clever man, and who was one of the disinterested friends so brilliant a woman as Hélène always has—men friends who can never change into lovers—once gave her his view of the matter at a small and intimate gathering.

"Listen, Bilíbin," said Hélène (she always called friends of that sort by their surnames), and she touched his coat sleeve with her white, beringed fingers. "Tell me, as you would a sister, what I ought to do. Which of the two?"

Bilíbin wrinkled up the skin over his eyebrows and pondered, with a smile on his lips.

"You are not taking me unawares, you know," said he. "As a true friend, I have thought and thought again about your affair. You see, if you marry the prince"—he meant the younger man—and he crooked one finger, "you forever lose the chance of marrying the other, and you will displease the court besides. (You know there is some kind of connection.) But if you marry the old count you will make his last days happy, and as widow of the Grand... the prince would no longer be making a *mésalliance* by marrying you," and Bilíbin smoothed out his forehead.

"That's a true friend!" said Hélène beaming, and again touching Bilíbin's sleeve. "But I love them, you know, and don't want to distress either of them. I would give my life for the happiness of them both."

Bilíbin shrugged his shoulders, as much as to say that not even he could help in that difficulty.

"*Une maîtresse-femme!* * That's what is called putting things squarely. She would like to be married to all three at the same time," thought he.

* A masterly woman.

"But tell me, how will your husband look at the matter?" Bilíbin asked, his reputation being so well established that he did not fear to ask so naïve a question. "Will he agree?"

"Oh, he loves me so!" said Hélène, who for some reason imagined that Pierre too loved her. "He will do anything for me."

Bilíbin puckered his skin in preparation for something witty.

"Even divorce you?" said he.

Hélène laughed.

Among those who ventured to doubt the justifiability of the proposed marriage was Hélène's mother, Princess Kurágina. She was continually tormented by jealousy of her daughter, and now that jealousy concerned a subject near to her own heart, she could not reconcile herself to the idea. She consulted a Russian priest as to the possibility of divorce and remarriage during a husband's lifetime, and the priest told her that it was impossible, and to her delight showed her a text in the Gospel which (as it seemed to him) plainly forbids remarriage while the husband is alive.

Armed with these arguments, which appeared to her unanswerable, she drove to her daughter's early one morning so as to find her alone.

Having listened to her mother's objections, Hélène smiled blandly and ironically.

"But it says plainly: 'Whosoever shall marry her that is divorced...'" said the old princess.

"Ah, Maman, ne dites pas de bêtises. Vous ne comprenezrien. Dans ma position j'ai des devoirs," * said Hélène changing from Russian, in which language she always felt that her case did not sound quite clear, into French which suited it better.

* "Oh, Mamma, don't talk nonsense! You don't understand anything. In my position I have obligations."

"But, my dear...."

"Oh, Mamma, how is it you don't understand that the Holy Father, who has the right to grant dispensations..."

Just then the lady companion who lived with Hélène came in to announce that His Highness was in the ballroom and wished to see her.

"Non, dites-lui que je ne veux pas le voir, que je suis furieuse contre lui, parcequ'il m'a manqué parole." *

* "No, tell him I don't wish to see him, I am furious with him for not keeping his word to me."

"Comtesse, à tout péché miséricorde," * said a fair-haired young man with a long face and nose, as he entered the room.

* "Countess, there is mercy for every sin."

The old princess rose respectfully and curtsied. The young man who had entered took no notice of her. The princess nodded to her daughter and sidled out of the room.

"Yes, she is right," thought the old princess, all her convictions dissipated by the appearance of His Highness. "She is right, but how is it that we in our irrecoverable youth did not know it? Yet it is so simple," she thought as she got into her carriage.

By the beginning of August Hélène's affairs were clearly defined and she wrote a letter to her husband—who, as she imagined, loved her very much—informing him of her intention to marry N.N. and of her having embraced the one true faith, and asking him to carry out all the formalities necessary for a divorce, which would be explained to him by the bearer of the letter.

And so I pray God to have you, my friend, in His holy and powerful keeping—Your friend Hélène.

This letter was brought to Pierre's house when he was on the field of Borodinó.

CHAPTER VIII

Toward the end of the battle of Borodinó, Pierre, having run down from Raévski's battery a second time, made his way through a gully to Knyazkóvo with a crowd of soldiers, reached the dressing station, and seeing blood and hearing cries and groans hurried on, still entangled in the crowds of soldiers.

The one thing he now desired with his whole soul was to get away quickly from the terrible sensations amid which he had lived that day and return to ordinary conditions of life and sleep quietly in a room in his own bed. He felt that only in the ordinary conditions of life would he be able to understand himself and all he had seen and felt. But such ordinary conditions of life were nowhere to be found.

Though shells and bullets did not whistle over the road along which he was going, still on all sides there was what there had been on the field of battle. There were still the same suffering, exhausted, and sometimes strangely indifferent faces, the same blood, the same soldiers' overcoats, the same sounds of firing which, though distant now, still aroused terror, and besides this there were the foul air and the dust.

Having gone a couple of miles along the Mozháysk road, Pierre sat down by the roadside.

Dusk had fallen, and the roar of guns died away. Pierre lay leaning on his elbow for a long time, gazing at the shadows that moved past him in the darkness. He was continually imagining that a cannon ball was flying toward him with a terrific whizz, and then he shuddered and sat up. He had no idea how long he had been there. In the middle of the night three soldiers, having brought some firewood, settled down near him and began lighting a fire.

The soldiers, who threw sidelong glances at Pierre, got the fire to burn and placed an iron pot on it into which they broke some dried bread and put a little dripping. The pleasant odor of greasy viands mingled with the smell of smoke. Pierre sat up and sighed. The three soldiers were eating and talking among themselves, taking no notice of him.

"And who may you be?" one of them suddenly asked Pierre, evidently meaning what Pierre himself had in mind, namely: "If you want to eat we'll give you some food, only let us know whether you are an honest man."

"I, I..." said Pierre, feeling it necessary to minimize his social position as much as possible so as to be nearer to the soldiers and better understood by them. "By rights I am a militia officer, but my men are not here. I came to the battle and have lost them."

"There now!" said one of the soldiers.

Another shook his head.

"Would you like a little mash?" the first soldier asked, and handed Pierre a wooden spoon after licking it clean.

Pierre sat down by the fire and began eating the mash, as they called the food in the cauldron, and he thought it more delicious than any food he had ever tasted. As he sat bending greedily over it, helping himself to large spoonfuls and chewing one after another, his face was lit up by the fire and the soldiers looked at him in silence.

"Where have you to go to? Tell us!" said one of them.

"To Mozháysk."

"You're a gentleman, aren't you?"

"Yes."

"And what's your name?"

"Peter Kirílych."

"Well then, Peter Kirílych, come along with us, we'll take you there."

In the total darkness the soldiers walked with Pierre to Mozháysk.

By the time they got near Mozháysk and began ascending the steep hill into the town, the cocks were already crowing. Pierre went on with the soldiers, quite forgetting that his inn was at the bottom of the hill and that he had already passed it. He would not soon have remembered this, such was his state of forgetfulness, had he not halfway up the hill stumbled upon his groom, who had been to look for him in the town and was returning to the inn. The groom recognized Pierre in the darkness by his white hat.

"Your excellency!" he said. "Why, we were beginning to despair! How is it you are on foot? And where are you going, please?"

"Oh, yes!" said Pierre.

The soldiers stopped.

"So you've found your folk?" said one of them. "Well, good-by, Peter Kirílych—isn't it?"

"Good-by, Peter Kirílych!" Pierre heard the other voices repeat.

"Good-by!" he said and turned with his groom toward the inn.

"I ought to give them something!" he thought, and felt in his pocket. "No, better not!" said another, inner voice.

There was not a room to be had at the inn, they were all occupied. Pierre went out into the yard and, covering himself up head and all, lay down in his carriage.

CHAPTER IX

S carcely had Pierre laid his head on the pillow before he felt himself falling asleep, but suddenly, almost with the distinctness of reality, he heard the *boom, boom, boom* of firing, the thud of projectiles, groans and cries, and smelled blood and powder, and a feeling of horror and dread of death seized him. Filled with fright he opened his eyes and lifted his head from under his cloak. All was tranquil in the yard. Only someone's orderly passed through the gateway, splashing through the mud, and talked to the innkeeper. Above Pierre's head some pigeons, disturbed by the movement he had made in sitting up, fluttered under the dark roof of the penthouse. The whole courtyard was permeated by a strong peaceful smell of stable yards, delightful to Pierre at that moment. He could see the clear starry sky between the dark roofs of two penthouses.

"Thank God, there is no more of that!" he thought, covering up his head again. "Oh, what a terrible thing is fear, and how shamefully I yielded to it! But they... *they* were steady and calm all the time, to the end..." thought he.

They, in Pierre's mind, were the soldiers, those who had been at the battery, those who had given him food, and those who had prayed before the icon. *They*, those strange men he had not previously known, stood out clearly and sharply from everyone else.

"To be a soldier, just a soldier!" thought Pierre as he fell asleep, "to enter communal life completely, to be imbued by what makes them what they are. But how to cast off all the superfluous, devilish burden of my outer man? There was a time when I could have done it. I could have run away from my father, as I wanted to. Or I might have been sent to serve as a soldier after the duel with Dólokhov." And the memory of the dinner at the English Club when he had challenged Dólokhov flashed through Pierre's mind, and then he remembered his benefactor at Torzhók. And now a picture of a solemn meeting of the lodge presented itself to his mind. It was taking place at the English Club and someone near and dear to him sat at the end of the table. "Yes, that is he! It is my benefactor. But he died!" thought Pierre. "Yes, he died, and I did not know he was alive. How sorry I am that he died, and how glad I am that he is alive again!" On one side of the table sat Anatole, Dólokhov, Nesvítski, Denísov, and others like them (in his dream the category to which these men belonged was as clearly defined in his mind as the category of those he termed *they*), and he heard those people, Anatole and Dólokhov, shouting and singing loudly; yet through their shouting the voice of his benefactor was heard speaking all the time and the sound of his words was as weighty and uninterrupted as the booming on the battlefield, but pleasant and comforting. Pierre did not understand what his benefactor was saying, but he knew (the categories of thoughts were also quite distinct in his dream) that he was talking of goodness and the possibility of being what *they* were. And *they* with their simple, kind, firm faces surrounded his benefactor on all sides. But though they were kindly they did not look at Pierre and did not know him. Wishing to speak and to attract their attention, he got up, but at that moment his legs grew cold and bare.

He felt ashamed, and with one arm covered his legs from which his cloak had in fact slipped. For a moment as he was rearranging his cloak Pierre opened his eyes and saw the same penthouse roofs, posts, and yard, but now they were all bluish, lit up, and glittering with frost or dew.

"It is dawn," thought Pierre. "But that's not what I want. I want to hear and understand my benefactor's words." Again he covered himself up with his cloak, but now neither the lodge nor his benefactor was there. There were only thoughts clearly expressed in words, thoughts that someone was uttering or that he himself was formulating.

Afterwards when he recalled those thoughts Pierre was convinced that someone outside himself had spoken them, though the impressions of that day had evoked them. He had never, it seemed to him, been able to think and express his thoughts like that when awake.

"To endure war is the most difficult subordination of man's freedom to the law of God," the voice had said. "Simplicity is submission to the will of God; you cannot escape from Him. And *they* are simple. *They* do not talk, but act. The spoken word is silver but the unspoken is golden. Man can be master of nothing while he fears death, but he who does not fear it possesses all. If there were no suffering, man would not know his limitations, would not know himself. The hardest thing (Pierre went on thinking, or hearing, in his dream) is to be able in your soul to unite the meaning of all. To unite all?" he asked himself. "No, not to unite. Thoughts cannot be united, but to *harness* all these thoughts together is what we need! Yes, one *must harness* them, *must harness* them!" he repeated to himself with inward rapture, feeling that these words and they alone expressed what he wanted to say and solved the question that tormented him.

"Yes, one must harness, it is time to harness."

"Time to harness, time to harness, your excellency! Your excellency!" some voice was repeating. "We must harness, it is time to harness...."

It was the voice of the groom, trying to wake him. The sun shone straight into Pierre's face. He glanced at the dirty innyard in the middle of which soldiers were watering their lean horses at the pump while carts were passing out of the gate. Pierre turned away with repugnance, and closing his eyes quickly fell back on the carriage seat. "No, I don't want that, I don't want to see and understand that. I want to understand what was revealing itself to me in my dream. One second more and I should have understood it all! But what am I to do? Harness, but how can I harness everything?" and Pierre felt with horror that the meaning of all he had seen and thought in the dream had been destroyed.

The groom, the coachman, and the innkeeper told Pierre that an officer had come with news that the French were already near Mozháysk and that our men were leaving it.

Pierre got up and, having told them to harness and overtake him, went on foot through the town.

The troops were moving on, leaving about ten thousand wounded behind them. There were wounded in the yards, at the windows of the houses, and the streets were crowded with them. In the streets, around carts that were to take some of the wounded away, shouts, curses, and blows could be heard. Pierre offered the use of his carriage, which had overtaken him, to a wounded general he knew, and drove with him to Moscow. On the way Pierre was told of the death of his brother-in-law Anatole and of that of Prince Andrew.

CHAPTER X

On the thirtieth of August Pierre reached Moscow. Close to the gates of the city he was met by Count Rostopchín's adjutant.

"We have been looking for you everywhere," said the adjutant. "The count wants to see you particularly. He asks you to come to him at once on a very important matter."

Without going home, Pierre took a cab and drove to see the Moscow commander in chief.

Count Rostopchín had only that morning returned to town from his summer villa at Sokólniki. The anteroom and reception room of his house were full of officials who had been summoned or had come for orders. Vasílchikov and Plátov had already seen the count and explained to him that it was impossible to defend Moscow and that it would have to be surrendered. Though this news was being concealed from the inhabitants, the officials—the heads of the various government departments—knew that Moscow would soon be in the enemy's hands, just as Count Rostopchín himself knew it, and to escape personal responsibility they had all come to the governor to ask how they were to deal with their various departments.

As Pierre was entering the reception room a courier from the army came out of Rostopchín's private room.

In answer to questions with which he was greeted, the courier made a despairing gesture with his hand and passed through the room.

While waiting in the reception room Pierre with weary eyes watched the various officials, old and young, military and civilian, who were there. They all seemed dissatisfied and uneasy. Pierre went up to a group of men, one of whom he knew. After greeting Pierre they continued their conversation.

"If they're sent out and brought back again later on it will do no harm, but as things are now one can't answer for anything."

"But you see what he writes..." said another, pointing to a printed sheet he held in his hand.

"That's another matter. That's necessary for the people," said the first.

"What is it?" asked Pierre.

"Oh, it's a fresh broadsheet."

Pierre took it and began reading.

His Serene Highness has passed through Mozháysk in order to join up with the troops moving toward him and has taken up a strong position where the enemy will not soon attack him. Forty-eight guns with ammunition have been sent him from here, and his Serene Highness says he will defend Moscow to the last drop of blood and is even ready to fight in the streets. Do not be upset, brothers, that the law courts are closed; things have to be put in order, and we will deal with villains in our own way! When the time comes I shall want both town and peasant lads and will raise the cry a day or two beforehand, but they are not wanted yet so I hold my peace. An ax will be useful, a hunting spear not bad, but a three-pronged fork will be best of all: a Frenchman is no heavier than a sheaf of rye. Tomorrow after dinner I shall take the Iberian icon of the Mother of God to the wounded in the Catherine Hospital where we will have some water blessed. That will help them to get well quicker. I, too, am well now: one of my eyes was sore but now I am on the lookout with both.

"But military men have told me that it is impossible to fight in the town," said Pierre, "and that the position..."

"Well, of course! That's what we were saying," replied the first speaker.

"And what does he mean by 'One of my eyes was sore but now I am on the lookout with both'?" asked Pierre.

"The count had a sty," replied the adjutant smiling, "and was very much upset when I told him people had come to ask what was the matter with him. By the by, Count," he added suddenly, addressing

Pierre with a smile, "we heard that you have family troubles and that the countess, your wife..."

"I have heard nothing," Pierre replied unconcernedly. "But what have you heard?"

"Oh, well, you know people often invent things. I only say what I heard."

"But what did you hear?"

"Well, they say," continued the adjutant with the same smile, "that the countess, your wife, is preparing to go abroad. I expect it's nonsense...."

"Possibly," remarked Pierre, looking about him absent-mindedly. "And who is that?" he asked, indicating a short old man in a clean blue peasant overcoat, with a big snow-white beard and eyebrows and a ruddy face.

"He? That's a tradesman, that is to say, he's the restaurant keeper, Vereshchágin. Perhaps you have heard of that affair with the proclamation."

"Oh, so that is Vereshchágin!" said Pierre, looking at the firm, calm face of the old man and seeking any indication of his being a traitor.

"That's not he himself, that's the father of the fellow who wrote the proclamation," said the adjutant. "The young man is in prison and I expect it will go hard with him."

An old gentleman wearing a star and another official, a German wearing a cross round his neck, approached the speaker.

"It's a complicated story, you know," said the adjutant. "That proclamation appeared about two months ago. The count was informed of it. He gave orders to investigate the matter. Gabriel Ivánovich here made the inquiries. The proclamation had passed through exactly sixty-three hands. He asked one, 'From whom did you get it?' 'From so-and-so.' He went to the next one. 'From whom did you get it?' and so on till he reached Vereshchágin, a half educated tradesman, you know, 'a pet of a trader,'" said the adjutant smiling. "They asked him, 'Who gave it you?' And the point is that we knew whom he had it from. He could only have had it from the Postmaster. But evidently they had come to some understanding. He replied: 'From no one; I made it up myself.' They threatened and questioned him, but he stuck to that: 'I made it up myself.' And so it was reported to the count, who sent for the man. 'From whom did you get the proclamation?' 'I wrote it myself.' Well, you know the count," said the adjutant cheerfully, with a smile of pride, "he flared up dreadfully— and just think of the fellow's audacity, lying, and obstinacy!"

"And the count wanted him to say it was from Klyucharëv? I understand!" said Pierre.

"Not at all," rejoined the adjutant in dismay. "Klyucharëv had his own sins to answer for without that and that is why he has been banished. But the point is that the count was much annoyed. 'How could you have written it yourself?' said he, and he took up the Hamburg *Gazette* that was lying on the table. 'Here it is! You did not write it yourself but translated it, and translated it abominably, because you don't even know French, you fool.' And what do you think? 'No,' said he, 'I have not read any papers, I made it up myself.' 'If that's so, you're a traitor and I'll have you tried, and you'll be hanged! Say from whom you had it.' 'I have seen no papers, I made it up myself.' And that was the end of it. The count had the father fetched, but the fellow stuck to it. He was sent for trial and condemned to hard labor, I believe. Now the father has come to intercede for him. But he's a good-for-nothing lad! You know that sort of tradesman's son, a dandy and lady-killer. He attended some lectures somewhere and imagines that the devil is no match for him. That's the sort of fellow he is. His father keeps a cookshop here by the Stone Bridge, and you know there was a large icon of God Almighty painted with a scepter in one hand and an orb in the other. Well, he took that icon home with him for a few days and what did he do? He found some scoundrel of a painter..."

CHAPTER XI

In the middle of this fresh tale Pierre was summoned to the commander in chief.

When he entered the private room Count Rostopchín, puckering his face, was rubbing his forehead and eyes with his hand. A short man was saying something, but when Pierre entered he stopped speaking and went out.

"Ah, how do you do, great warrior?" said Rostopchín as soon as the short man had left the room. "We have heard of your prowess. But that's not the point. Between ourselves, *moncher*, do you belong to the Masons?" he went on severely, as though there were something wrong about it which he nevertheless intended to pardon. Pierre remained silent. "I am well informed, my friend, but I am aware that there are Masons and I hope that you are not one of those who on pretense of saving mankind wish to ruin Russia."

"Yes, I am a Mason," Pierre replied.

"There, you see, *moncher!* I expect you know that Messrs. Speránski and Magnítski have been deported to their proper place. Mr. Klyucharëv has been treated in the same way, and so have others who on the plea of building up the temple of Solomon have tried to destroy the temple of their fatherland. You can understand that there are reasons for this and that I could not have exiled the Postmaster had he not been a harmful person. It has now come to my knowledge that you lent him your carriage for his removal from town, and that you have even accepted papers from him for safe custody. I like you and don't wish you any harm and—as you are only half my age—I advise you, as a father would, to cease all communication with men of that stamp and to leave here as soon as possible."

"But what did Klyucharëv do wrong, Count?" asked Pierre.

"That is for me to know, but not for you to ask," shouted Rostopchín.

"If he is accused of circulating Napoleon's proclamation it is not proved that he did so," said Pierre without looking at Rostopchín, "and Vereshchágin..."

"There we are!" Rostopchín shouted at Pierre louder than before, frowning suddenly. "Vereshchágin is a renegade and a traitor who will be punished as he deserves," said he with the vindictive heat with which people speak when recalling an insult. "But I did not summon you to discuss my actions, but to give you advice—or an order if you prefer it. I beg you to leave the town and break off all communication with such men as Klyucharëv. And I will knock the nonsense out of anybody"—but probably realizing that he was shouting at Bezúkhov who so far was not guilty of anything, he added, taking Pierre's hand in a friendly manner, "We are on the eve of a public disaster and I haven't time to be polite to everybody who has business with me. My head is sometimes in a whirl. Well, *moncher*, what are you doing personally?"

"Why, nothing," answered Pierre without raising his eyes or changing the thoughtful expression of his face.

The count frowned.

"A word of friendly advice, *moncher*. Be off as soon as you can, that's all I have to tell you. Happy he who has ears to hear. Good-by, my dear fellow. Oh, by the by!" he shouted through the doorway after Pierre, "is it true that the countess has fallen into the clutches of the holy fathers of the Society of Jesus?"

Pierre did not answer and left Rostopchín's room more sullen and angry than he had ever before shown himself.

When he reached home it was already getting dark. Some eight people had come to see him that evening: the secretary of a committee, the colonel of his battalion, his steward, his major-domo, and various petitioners. They all had business with Pierre and wanted decisions from him. Pierre did not understand and was not interested in any of these questions and only answered them in order to get rid of these people. When left alone at last he opened and read his wife's letter.

"*They*, the soldiers at the battery, Prince Andrew killed... that old man... Simplicity is submission to God. Suffering is necessary... the meaning of all... one must harness... my wife is getting married... One must forget and understand..." And going to his bed he threw himself on it without undressing and immediately fell asleep.

When he awoke next morning the major-domo came to inform him that a special messenger, a police officer, had come from Count Rostopchín to know whether Count Bezúkhov had left or was leaving the town.

A dozen persons who had business with Pierre were awaiting him in the drawing room. Pierre dressed hurriedly and, instead of going to see them, went to the back porch and out through the gate.

From that time till the end of the destruction of Moscow no one of Bezúkhov's household, despite all the search they made, saw Pierre again or knew where he was.

CHAPTER XII

The Rostóvs remained in Moscow till the first of September, that is, till the eve of the enemy's entry into the city.

After Pétya had joined Obolénski's regiment of Cossacks and left for BélayaTsérkov where that regiment was forming, the countess was seized with terror. The thought that both her sons were at the war, had both gone from under her wing, that today or tomorrow either or both of them might be killed like the three sons of one of her acquaintances, struck her that summer for the first time with cruel clearness. She tried to get Nicholas back and wished to go herself to join Pétya, or to get him an appointment somewhere in Petersburg, but neither of these proved possible. Pétya could not return unless his regiment did so or unless he was transferred to another regiment on active service. Nicholas was somewhere with the army and had not sent a word since his last letter, in which he had given a detailed account of his meeting with Princess Mary. The countess did not sleep at night, or when she did fall asleep dreamed that she saw her sons lying dead. After many consultations and conversations, the count at last devised means to tranquillize her. He got Pétya transferred from Obolénski's regiment to Bezúkhov's, which was in training near Moscow. Though Pétya would remain in the service, this transfer would give the countess the consolation of seeing at least one of her sons under her wing, and she hoped to arrange matters for her Pétya so as not to let him go again, but always get him appointed to places where he could not possibly take part in a battle. As long as Nicholas alone was in danger the countess imagined that she loved her first-born more than all her other children and even reproached herself for it; but when her youngest: the scapegrace who had been bad at lessons, was always breaking things in the house and making himself a nuisance to everybody, that snub-nosed Pétya with his merry black eyes and fresh rosy cheeks where soft down was just beginning to show—when he was thrown amid those big, dreadful, cruel men who were fighting somewhere about something and apparently finding pleasure in it—then his mother thought she loved him more, much more, than all her other children. The nearer the time came for Pétya to return, the more uneasy grew the countess. She began to think she would never live to see such happiness. The presence of Sónya, of her beloved Natásha, or even of her husband irritated her. "What do I want with them? I want no one but Pétya," she thought.

At the end of August the Rostóvs received another letter from Nicholas. He wrote from the province of Vorónezh where he had been sent to procure remounts, but that letter did not set the countess at ease. Knowing that one son was out of danger she became the more anxious about Pétya.

Though by the twentieth of August nearly all the Rostóvs' acquaintances had left Moscow, and though everybody tried to persuade the countess to get away as quickly as possible, she would not hear of leaving before her treasure, her adored Pétya, returned. On the twenty-eighth of August he arrived. The passionate tenderness with which his mother received him did not please the sixteen-year-old officer. Though she concealed from him her intention of keeping him under her wing, Pétya guessed her designs, and instinctively fearing that he might give way to emotion when with her—might "become womanish" as he termed it to himself—he treated her coldly, avoided her, and during his stay in Moscow attached himself exclusively to Natásha for whom he had always had a particularly brotherly tenderness, almost lover-like.

Owing to the count's customary carelessness nothing was ready for their departure by the twenty-eighth of August and the carts that were to come from their Ryazán and Moscow estates to remove their household belongings did not arrive till the thirtieth.

From the twenty-eighth till the thirty-first all Moscow was in a bustle and commotion. Every day thousands of men wounded at Borodinó were brought in by the Dorogomílov gate and taken to various parts of Moscow, and thousands of carts conveyed the inhabitants and their possessions out by the other gates. In spite of Rostopchín's broadsheets, or because of them or independently of them, the strangest and most contradictory rumors were current in the town. Some said that no one was to be allowed to leave the city, others on the contrary said that all the icons had been taken out of the churches and everybody was to be ordered to leave. Some said there had been another battle after Borodinó at which the French had been routed, while others on the contrary reported that the Russian army had been destroyed. Some talked about the Moscow militia which, preceded by the clergy, would go to the Three Hills; others whispered that Augustin had been forbidden to leave, that traitors had been seized, that the peasants were rioting and robbing people on their way from Moscow, and so on. But all this was only talk; in reality (though the Council of Filí, at which it was decided to abandon Moscow, had not yet been held) both those who went away and those who remained behind felt, though they did not show it, that Moscow would certainly be abandoned, and that they ought to get away as quickly as possible and save their belongings. It was felt that everything would suddenly break up and change, but up to the first of September nothing had done so. As a criminal who is being led to execution knows that he must die immediately, but yet looks about him and straightens the cap that is awry on his head, so Moscow involuntarily continued its wonted life, though it knew that the time of its destruction was near when the conditions of life to which its people were accustomed to submit would be completely upset.

During the three days preceding the occupation of Moscow the whole Rostóv family was absorbed in various activities. The head of the family, Count IlyáRostóv, continually drove about the city collecting the current rumors from all sides and gave superficial and hasty orders at home about the preparations for their departure.

The countess watched the things being packed, was dissatisfied with everything, was constantly in pursuit of Pétya who was always running away from her, and was jealous of Natásha with whom he spent all his time. Sónya alone directed the practical side of matters by getting things packed. But of late Sónya had been particularly sad and silent. Nicholas' letter in which he mentioned Princess Mary had elicited, in her presence, joyous comments from the countess, who saw an intervention of Providence in this meeting of the princess and Nicholas.

"I was never pleased at Bolkónski's engagement to Natásha," said the countess, "but I always wanted Nicholas to marry the princess, and had a presentiment that it would happen. What a good thing it would be!"

Sónya felt that this was true: that the only possibility of retrieving the Rostóvs' affairs was by Nicholas marrying a rich woman, and that the princess was a good match. It was very bitter for her. But despite her grief, or perhaps just because of it, she took on herself all the difficult work of directing the storing and packing of their things and was busy for whole days. The count and countess turned to her when they had any orders to give. Pétya and Natásha on the contrary, far from helping their parents, were generally a nuisance and a hindrance to everyone. Almost all day long the house resounded with their running feet, their cries, and their spontaneous laughter. They laughed and were gay not because there was any reason to laugh, but because gaiety and mirth were in their hearts and so everything that happened was a cause for gaiety and laughter to them. Pétya was in high spirits because having left home a boy he had returned (as everybody told him) a fine young man, because he was at home, because he had left BélayaTsérkov where there was no hope of soon taking part in a battle and had come to Moscow where there was to be fighting in a few days, and chiefly because Natásha, whose lead he always followed, was in high spirits. Natásha was gay because she had been sad too long and now nothing reminded her of the cause of her sadness, and because she was feeling well. She was also happy because she had someone to adore her: the adoration of others was a lubricant the wheels of her machine needed to make them run freely—and Pétya adored her. Above all, they were gay because there was a war near Moscow, there would be fighting at the town gates, arms were being given out, everybody was escaping—going away somewhere, and in general something extraordinary was happening, and that is always exciting, especially to the young.

CHAPTER XIII

On Saturday, the thirty-first of August, everything in the Rostóvs' house seemed topsy-turvy. All the doors were open, all the furniture was being carried out or moved about, and the mirrors and pictures had been taken down. There were trunks in the rooms, and hay, wrapping paper, and ropes were scattered about. The peasants and house serfs carrying out the things were treading heavily on the parquet floors. The yard was crowded with peasant carts, some loaded high and already corded up, others still empty.

The voices and footsteps of the many servants and of the peasants who had come with the carts resounded as they shouted to one another in the yard and in the house. The count had been out since morning. The countess had a headache brought on by all the noise and turmoil and was lying down in the new sitting room with a vinegar compress on her head. Pétya was not at home, he had gone to visit a friend with whom he meant to obtain a transfer from the militia to the active army. Sónya was in the ballroom looking after the packing of the glass and china. Natásha was sitting on the floor of her dismantled room with dresses, ribbons, and scarves strewn all about her, gazing fixedly at the floor and holding in her hands the old ball dress (already out of fashion) which she had worn at her first Petersburg ball.

Natásha was ashamed of doing nothing when everyone else was so busy, and several times that morning had tried to set to work, but her heart was not in it, and she could not and did not know how to do anything except with all her heart and all her might. For a while she had stood beside Sónya while the china was being packed and tried to help, but soon gave it up and went to her room to pack her own things. At first she found it amusing to give away dresses and ribbons to the maids, but when that was done and what was left had still to be packed, she found it dull.

"Dunyásha, you pack! You will, won't you, dear?" And when Dunyásha willingly promised to do it all for her, Natásha sat down on the floor, took her old ball dress, and fell into a reverie quite unrelated to what ought to have occupied her thoughts now. She was roused from her reverie by the talk of the maids in the next room (which was theirs) and by the sound of their hurried footsteps going to the back porch. Natásha got up and looked out of the window. An enormously long row of carts full of wounded men had stopped in the street.

The housekeeper, the old nurse, the cooks, coachmen, maids, footmen, postilions, and scullions stood at the gate, staring at the wounded.

Natásha, throwing a clean pocket handkerchief over her hair and holding an end of it in each hand, went out into the street.

The former housekeeper, old MávraKuzmínichna, had stepped out of the crowd by the gate, gone up to a cart with a hood constructed of bast mats, and was speaking to a pale young officer who lay inside. Natásha moved a few steps forward and stopped shyly, still holding her handkerchief, and listened to what the housekeeper was saying.

"Then you have nobody in Moscow?" she was saying. "You would be more comfortable somewhere in a house... in ours, for instance... the family are leaving."

"I don't know if it would be allowed," replied the officer in a weak voice. "Here is our commanding officer... ask him," and he pointed to a stout major who was walking back along the street past the row of carts.

Natásha glanced with frightened eyes at the face of the wounded officer and at once went to meet the major.

"May the wounded men stay in our house?" she asked.

The major raised his hand to his cap with a smile.

"Which one do you want, Ma'am'selle?" said he, screwing up his eyes and smiling.

Natásha quietly repeated her question, and her face and whole manner were so serious, though she was still holding the ends of her handkerchief, that the major ceased smiling and after some reflection—as if considering in how far the thing was possible—replied in the affirmative.

"Oh yes, why not? They may," he said.

With a slight inclination of her head, Natásha stepped back quickly to MávraKuzmínichna, who stood talking compassionately to the officer.

"They may. He says they may!" whispered Natásha.

The cart in which the officer lay was turned into the Rostóvs' yard, and dozens of carts with wounded men began at the invitation of the townsfolk to turn into the yards and to draw up at the entrances of the houses in Povarskáya Street. Natásha was evidently pleased to be dealing with new people outside the ordinary routine of her life. She and MávraKuzmínichna tried to get as many of the wounded as possible into their yard.

"Your Papa must be told, though," said MávraKuzmínichna.

"Never mind, never mind, what does it matter? For one day we can move into the drawing room. They can have all our half of the house."

"There now, young lady, you do take things into your head! Even if we put them into the wing, the men's room, or the nurse's room, we must ask permission."

"Well, I'll ask."

Natásha ran into the house and went on tiptoe through the half-open door into the sitting room, where there was a smell of vinegar and Hoffman's drops.

"Are you asleep, Mamma?"

"Oh, what sleep—?" said the countess, waking up just as she was dropping into a doze.

"Mamma darling!" said Natásha, kneeling by her mother and bringing her face close to her mother's, "I am sorry, forgive me, I'll never do it again; I woke you up! MávraKuzmínichna has sent me: they have brought some wounded here—officers. Will you let them come? They have nowhere to go. I knew you'd let them come!" she said quickly all in one breath.

"What officers? Whom have they brought? I don't understand anything about it," said the countess.

Natásha laughed, and the countess too smiled slightly.

"I knew you'd give permission... so I'll tell them," and, having kissed her mother, Natásha got up and went to the door.

In the hall she met her father, who had returned with bad news.

"We've stayed too long!" said the count with involuntary vexation. "The Club is closed and the police are leaving."

"Papa, is it all right—I've invited some of the wounded into the house?" said Natásha.

"Of course it is," he answered absently. "That's not the point. I beg you not to indulge in trifles now, but to help to pack, and tomorrow we must go, go, go!..."

And the count gave a similar order to the major-domo and the servants.

At dinner Pétya having returned home told them the news he had heard. He said the people had been getting arms in the Krémlin, and that though Rostopchín's broadsheet had said that he would sound a call two or three days in advance, the order had certainly already been given for everyone to go armed to the Three Hills tomorrow, and that there would be a big battle there.

The countess looked with timid horror at her son's eager, excited face as he said this. She realized that if she said a word about his not going to the battle (she knew he enjoyed the thought of the impending engagement) he would say something about men, honor, and the fatherland—something senseless, masculine, and obstinate which there would be no contradicting, and her plans would be spoiled; and so, hoping to arrange to leave before then and take Pétya with her as their protector and defender, she did not answer him, but after dinner called the count aside and implored him with tears to take her away quickly, that very night if possible. With a woman's involuntary loving cunning she, who till then had not shown any alarm, said that she would die of fright if they did not leave that very night. Without any pretense she was now afraid of everything.

CHAPTER XIV

Madame Schoss, who had been out to visit her daughter, increased the countess' fears still more by telling what she had seen at a spirit dealer's in Myasnítski Street. When returning by that street she had been unable to pass because of a drunken crowd rioting in front of the shop. She had taken a cab and driven home by a side street and the cabman had told her that the people were breaking open the barrels at the drink store, having received orders to do so.

After dinner the whole Rostóv household set to work with enthusiastic haste packing their belongings and preparing for their departure. The old count, suddenly setting to work, kept passing from the yard to the house and back again, shouting confused instructions to the hurrying people, and flurrying them still more. Pétya directed things in the yard. Sónya, owing to the count's contradictory orders, lost her head and did not know what to do. The servants ran noisily about the house and yard, shouting and disputing. Natásha, with the ardor characteristic of all she did suddenly set to work too. At first her intervention in the business of packing was received skeptically. Everybody expected some prank from her and did not wish to obey her; but she resolutely and passionately demanded obedience, grew angry and nearly cried because they did not heed her, and at last succeeded in making them believe her. Her first exploit, which cost her immense effort and established her authority, was the packing of the carpets. The count had valuable Gobelin tapestries and Persian carpets in the house. When Natásha set to work two cases were standing open in the ballroom, one almost full up with crockery, the other with carpets. There was also much china standing on the tables, and still more was being brought in from the storeroom. A third case was needed and servants had gone to fetch it.

"Sónya, wait a bit—we'll pack everything into these," said Natásha.

"You can't, Miss, we have tried to," said the butler's assistant.

"No, wait a minute, please."

And Natásha began rapidly taking out of the case dishes and plates wrapped in paper.

"The dishes must go in here among the carpets," said she.

"Why, it's a mercy if we can get the carpets alone into three cases," said the butler's assistant.

"Oh, wait, please!" And Natásha began rapidly and deftly sorting out the things. "These aren't needed," said she, putting aside some plates of Kiev ware. "These—yes, these must go among the carpets," she said, referring to the Saxony china dishes.

"Don't, Natásha! Leave it alone! We'll get it all packed," urged Sónya reproachfully.

"What a young lady she is!" remarked the major-domo.

But Natásha would not give in. She turned everything out and began quickly repacking, deciding that the inferior Russian carpets and unnecessary crockery should not be taken at all. When everything had been taken out of the cases, they recommenced packing, and it turned out that when the cheaper things not worth taking had nearly all been rejected, the valuable ones really did all go into the two cases. Only the lid of the case containing the carpets would not shut down. A few more things might have been taken out, but Natásha insisted on having her own way. She packed, repacked, pressed, made the butler's assistant and Pétya—whom she had drawn into the business of packing—press on the lid, and made desperate efforts herself.

"That's enough, Natásha," said Sónya. "I see you were right, but just take out the top one."

"I won't!" cried Natásha, with one hand holding back the hair that hung over her perspiring face, while with the other she pressed down the carpets. "Now press, Pétya! Press, Vasílich, press hard!" she cried.

The carpets yielded and the lid closed; Natásha, clapping her hands, screamed with delight and tears fell from her eyes. But this only lasted a moment. She at once set to work afresh and they now trusted her completely. The count was not angry even when they told him that Natásha had countermanded an order of his, and the servants now came to her to ask whether a cart was sufficiently loaded, and whether it might be corded up. Thanks to Natásha's directions the work now went on expeditiously, unnecessary things were left, and the most valuable packed as compactly as possible.

But hard as they all worked till quite late that night, they could not get everything packed. The countess had fallen asleep and the count, having put off their departure till next morning, went to bed.

Sónya and Natásha slept in the sitting room without undressing.

That night another wounded man was driven down the Povarskáya, and MávraKuzmínichna, who was standing at the gate, had him brought into the Rostóvs' yard. MávraKuzmínichna concluded that he was a very important man. He was being conveyed in a *calèche* with a raised hood, and was quite covered by an apron. On the box beside the driver sat a venerable old attendant. A doctor and two soldiers followed the carriage in a cart.

"Please come in here. The masters are going away and the whole house will be empty," said the old woman to the old attendant.

"Well, perhaps," said he with a sigh. "We don't expect to get him home alive! We have a house of our own in Moscow, but it's a long way from here, and there's nobody living in it."

"Do us the honor to come in, there's plenty of everything in the master's house. Come in," said MávraKuzmínichna. "Is he very ill?" she asked.

The attendant made a hopeless gesture.

"We don't expect to get him home! We must ask the doctor."

And the old servant got down from the box and went up to the cart.

"All right!" said the doctor.

The old servant returned to the *calèche*, looked into it, shook his head disconsolately, told the driver to turn into the yard, and stopped beside MávraKuzmínichna.

"O, Lord Jesus Christ!" she murmured.

She invited them to take the wounded man into the house.

"The masters won't object..." she said.

But they had to avoid carrying the man upstairs, and so they took him into the wing and put him in the room that had been Madame Schoss'.

This wounded man was Prince Andrew Bolkónski.

CHAPTER XV

Moscow's last day had come. It was a clear bright autumn day, a Sunday. The church bells everywhere were ringing for service, just as usual on Sundays. Nobody seemed yet to realize what awaited the city.

Only two things indicated the social condition of Moscow—the rabble, that is the poor people, and the price of commodities. An enormous crowd of factory hands, house serfs, and peasants, with whom some officials, seminarists, and gentry were mingled, had gone early that morning to the Three Hills. Having waited there for Rostopchín who did not turn up, they became convinced that Moscow would be surrendered, and then dispersed all about the town to the public houses and cookshops. Prices too that day indicated the state of affairs. The price of weapons, of gold, of carts and horses, kept rising, but the value of paper money and city articles kept falling, so that by midday there were instances of carters removing valuable goods, such as cloth, and receiving in payment a half of what they carted, while peasant horses were fetching five hundred rubles each, and furniture, mirrors, and bronzes were being given away for nothing.

In the Rostóvs' staid old-fashioned house the dissolution of former conditions of life was but little noticeable. As to the serfs the only indication was that three out of their huge retinue disappeared during the night, but nothing was stolen; and as to the value of their possessions, the thirty peasant carts that had come in from their estates and which many people envied proved to be extremely valuable and they were offered enormous sums of money for them. Not only were huge sums offered for the horses and carts, but on the previous evening and early in the morning of the first of September, orderlies and servants sent by wounded officers came to the Rostóvs' and wounded men dragged themselves there from the Rostóvs' and from neighboring houses where they were accommodated, entreating the servants to try to get them a lift out of Moscow. The major-domo to whom these entreaties were addressed, though he was sorry for the wounded, resolutely refused, saying that he dare not even mention the matter to the count. Pity these wounded men as one might, it was evident that if they were given one cart there would be no reason to refuse another, or all the carts and one's own carriages as well. Thirty carts could not save all the wounded and in the general catastrophe one could not disregard oneself and one's own family. So thought the major-domo on his master's behalf.

On waking up that morning Count IlyáRostóv left his bedroom softly, so as not to wake the countess who had fallen asleep only toward morning, and came out to the porch in his lilac silk dressing gown. In the yard stood the carts ready corded. The carriages were at the front porch. The major-domo stood at the porch talking to an elderly orderly and to a pale young officer with a bandaged arm. On seeing the count the major-domo made a significant and stern gesture to them both to go away.

"Well, Vasílich, is everything ready?" asked the count, and stroking his bald head he looked good-naturedly at the officer and the orderly and nodded to them. (He liked to see new faces.)

"We can harness at once, your excellency."

"Well, that's right. As soon as the countess wakes we'll be off, God willing! What is it, gentlemen?" he added, turning to the officer. "Are you staying in my house?"

The officer came nearer and suddenly his face flushed crimson.

"Count, be so good as to allow me... for God's sake, to get into some corner of one of your carts! I have nothing here with me.... I shall be all right on a loaded cart...."

Before the officer had finished speaking the orderly made the same request on behalf of his master.

"Oh, yes, yes, yes!" said the count hastily. "I shall be very pleased, very pleased. Vasílich, you'll see to it. Just unload one or two carts. Well, what of it... do what's necessary..." said the count, muttering some indefinite order.

But at the same moment an expression of warm gratitude on the officer's face had already sealed the order. The count looked around him. In the yard, at the gates, at the window of the wings, wounded officers and their orderlies were to be seen. They were all looking at the count and moving toward the porch.

"Please step into the gallery, your excellency," said the major-domo. "What are your orders about the pictures?"

The count went into the house with him, repeating his order not to refuse the wounded who asked for a lift.

"Well, never mind, some of the things can be unloaded," he added in a soft, confidential voice, as though afraid of being overheard.

At nine o'clock the countess woke up, and MatrënaTimoféevna, who had been her lady's maid before her marriage and now performed a sort of chief gendarme's duty for her, came to say that Madame Schoss was much offended and the young ladies' summer dresses could not be left behind. On inquiry, the countess learned that Madame Schoss was offended because her trunk had been taken down from its cart, and all the loads were being uncorded and the luggage taken out of the carts to make room for wounded men whom the count in the simplicity of his heart had ordered that they should take with them. The countess sent for her husband.

"What is this, my dear? I hear that the luggage is being unloaded."

"You know, love, I wanted to tell you... Countess dear... an officer came to me to ask for a few carts for the wounded. After all, ours are things that can be bought but think what being left behind means to them!... Really now, in our own yard—we asked them in ourselves and there are officers among them.... You know, I think, my dear... let them be taken... where's the hurry?"

The count spoke timidly, as he always did when talking of money matters. The countess was accustomed to this tone as a precursor of news of something detrimental to the children's interests, such as the building of a new gallery or conservatory, the inauguration of a private theater or an orchestra. She was accustomed always to oppose anything announced in that timid tone and considered it her duty to do so.

She assumed her dolefully submissive manner and said to her husband: "Listen to me, Count, you have managed matters so that we are getting nothing for the house, and now you wish to throw away all our—all *the children's* property! You said yourself that we have a hundred thousand rubles' worth of things in the house. I don't consent, my dear, I don't! Do as you please! It's the government's business to look after the wounded; they know that. Look at the Lopukhíns opposite, they cleared out everything two days ago. That's what other people do. It's only we who are such fools. If you have no pity on me, have some for the children."

Flourishing his arms in despair the count left the room without replying.

"Papa, what are you doing that for?" asked Natásha, who had followed him into her mother's room.

"Nothing! What business is it of yours?" muttered the count angrily.

"But I heard," said Natásha. "Why does Mamma object?"

"What business is it of yours?" cried the count.

Natásha stepped up to the window and pondered.

"Papa! Here's Berg coming to see us," said she, looking out of the window.

CHAPTER XVI

Berg, the Rostóvs' son-in-law, was already a colonel wearing the orders of Vladímir and Anna, and he still filled the quiet and agreeable post of assistant to the head of the staff of the assistant commander of the first division of the Second Army.

On the first of September he had come to Moscow from the army.

He had nothing to do in Moscow, but he had noticed that everyone in the army was asking for leave to visit Moscow and had something to do there. So he considered it necessary to ask for leave of absence for family and domestic reasons.

Berg drove up to his father-in-law's house in his spruce little trap with a pair of sleek roans, exactly like those of a certain prince. He looked attentively at the carts in the yard and while going up to the porch took out a clean pocket handkerchief and tied a knot in it.

From the anteroom Berg ran with smooth though impatient steps into the drawing room, where he embraced the count, kissed the hands of Natásha and Sónya, and hastened to inquire after "Mamma's" health.

"Health, at a time like this?" said the count. "Come, tell us the news! Is the army retreating or will there be another battle?"

"God Almighty alone can decide the fate of our fatherland, Papa," said Berg. "The army is burning with a spirit of heroism and the leaders, so to say, have now assembled in council. No one knows what is coming. But in general I can tell you, Papa, that such a heroic spirit, the truly antique valor of the Russian army, which they—which it" (he corrected himself) "has shown or displayed in the battle of the twenty-sixth—there are no words worthy to do it justice! I tell you, Papa" (he smote himself on the breast as a general he had heard speaking had done, but Berg did it a trifle late for he should have struck his breast at the words "Russian army"), "I tell you frankly that we, the commanders, far from having to urge the men on or anything of that kind, could hardly restrain those... those... yes, those exploits of antique valor," he went on rapidly. "General Barclay de Tolly risked his life everywhere at the head of the troops, I can assure you. Our corps was stationed on a hillside. You can imagine!"

And Berg related all that he remembered of the various tales he had heard those days. Natásha watched him with an intent gaze that confused him, as if she were trying to find in his face the answer to some question.

"Altogether such heroism as was displayed by the Russian warriors cannot be imagined or adequately praised!" said Berg, glancing round at Natásha, and as if anxious to conciliate her, replying to her intent look with a smile. "'Russia is not in Moscow, she lives in the hearts of her sons!' Isn't it so, Papa?" said he.

Just then the countess came in from the sitting room with a weary and dissatisfied expression. Berg hurriedly jumped up, kissed her hand, asked about her health, and, swaying his head from side to side to express sympathy, remained standing beside her.

"Yes, Mamma, I tell you sincerely that these are hard and sad times for every Russian. But why are you so anxious? You have still time to get away...."

"I can't think what the servants are about," said the countess, turning to her husband. "I have just been told that nothing is ready yet. Somebody after all must see to things. One misses Mítenka at such times. There won't be any end to it."

The count was about to say something, but evidently restrained himself. He got up from his chair and went to the door.

At that moment Berg drew out his handkerchief as if to blow his nose and, seeing the knot in it, pondered, shaking his head sadly and significantly.

"And I have a great favor to ask of you, Papa," said he.

"Hm..." said the count, and stopped.

"I was driving past Yusúpov's house just now," said Berg with a laugh, "when the steward, a man I know, ran out and asked me whether I wouldn't buy something. I went in out of curiosity, you know, and there is a small chiffonier and a dressing table. You know how dear Véra wanted a chiffonier like that and how we had a dispute about it." (At the mention of the chiffonier and dressing table Berg involuntarily changed his tone to one of pleasure at his admirable domestic arrangements.) "And it's such a beauty! It pulls out and has a secret English drawer, you know! And dear Véra has long wanted one. I wish to give her a surprise, you see. I saw so many of those peasant carts in your yard. Please let me have one, I will pay the man well, and..."

The count frowned and coughed.

"Ask the countess, I don't give orders."

"If it's inconvenient, please don't," said Berg. "Only I so wanted it, for dear Véra's sake."

"Oh, go to the devil, all of you! To the devil, the devil, the devil..." cried the old count. "My head's in a whirl!"

And he left the room. The countess began to cry.

"Yes, Mamma! Yes, these are very hard times!" said Berg.

Natásha left the room with her father and, as if finding it difficult to reach some decision, first followed him and then ran downstairs.

Pétya was in the porch, engaged in giving out weapons to the servants who were to leave Moscow. The loaded carts were still standing in the yard. Two of them had been uncorded and a wounded officer was climbing into one of them helped by an orderly.

"Do you know what it's about?" Pétya asked Natásha.

She understood that he meant what were their parents quarreling about. She did not answer.

"It's because Papa wanted to give up all the carts to the wounded," said Pétya. "Vasílich told me. I consider..."

"I consider," Natásha suddenly almost shouted, turning her angry face to Pétya, "I consider it so horrid, so abominable, so... I don't know what. Are we despicable Germans?"

Her throat quivered with convulsive sobs and, afraid of weakening and letting the force of her anger run to waste, she turned and rushed headlong up the stairs.

Berg was sitting beside the countess consoling her with the respectful attention of a relative. The count, pipe in hand, was pacing up and down the room, when Natásha, her face distorted by anger, burst in like a tempest and approached her mother with rapid steps.

"It's horrid! It's abominable!" she screamed. "You can't possibly have ordered it!"

Berg and the countess looked at her, perplexed and frightened. The count stood still at the window and listened.

"Mamma, it's impossible: see what is going on in the yard!" she cried. "They will be left!..."

"What's the matter with you? Who are 'they'? What do you want?"

"Why, the wounded! It's impossible, Mamma. It's monstrous!... No, Mamma darling, it's not the thing. Please forgive me, darling.... Mamma, what does it matter what we take away? Only look what is going on in the yard... Mamma!... It's impossible!"

The count stood by the window and listened without turning round. Suddenly he sniffed and put his face closer to the window.

The countess glanced at her daughter, saw her face full of shame for her mother, saw her agitation, and understood why her husband did not turn to look at her now, and she glanced round quite disconcerted.

"Oh, do as you like! Am I hindering anyone?" she said, not surrendering at once.

"Mamma, darling, forgive me!"

But the countess pushed her daughter away and went up to her husband.

"My dear, you order what is right.... You know I don't understand about it," said she, dropping her eyes shamefacedly.

"The eggs... the eggs are teaching the hen," muttered the count through tears of joy, and he embraced his wife who was glad to hide her look of shame on his breast.

"Papa! Mamma! May I see to it? May I?..." asked Natásha. "We will still take all the most necessary things."

The count nodded affirmatively, and Natásha, at the rapid pace at which she used to run when playing at tag, ran through the ballroom to the anteroom and downstairs into the yard.

The servants gathered round Natásha, but could not believe the strange order she brought them until the count himself, in his wife's name, confirmed the order to give up all the carts to the wounded and take the trunks to the storerooms. When they understood that order the servants set to work at this new task with pleasure and zeal. It no longer seemed strange to them but on the contrary it seemed the only thing that could be done, just as a quarter of an hour before it had not seemed strange to anyone that the wounded should be left behind and the goods carted away but that had seemed the only thing to do.

The whole household, as if to atone for not having done it sooner, set eagerly to work at the new task of placing the wounded in the carts. The wounded dragged themselves out of their rooms and stood with pale but happy faces round the carts. The news that carts were to be had spread to the neighboring houses, from which wounded men began to come into the Rostóvs' yard. Many of the wounded asked them not to unload the carts but only to let them sit on the top of the things. But the work of unloading, once started, could not be arrested. It seemed not to matter whether all or only half the things were left behind. Cases full of china, bronzes, pictures, and mirrors that had been so carefully packed the night before now lay about the yard, and still they went on searching for and finding possibilities of unloading this or that and letting the wounded have another and yet another cart.

"We can take four more men," said the steward. "They can have my trap, or else what is to become of them?"

"Let them have my wardrobe cart," said the countess. "Dunyásha can go with me in the carriage."

They unloaded the wardrobe cart and sent it to take wounded men from a house two doors off. The whole household, servants included, was bright and animated. Natásha was in a state of rapturous excitement such as she had not known for a long time.

"What could we fasten this onto?" asked the servants, trying to fix a trunk on the narrow footboard behind a carriage. "We must keep at least one cart."

"What's in it?" asked Natásha.

"The count's books."

"Leave it, Vasílich will put it away. It's not wanted."

The phaeton was full of people and there was a doubt as to where Count Peter could sit.

"On the box. You'll sit on the box, won't you, Pétya?" cried Natásha.

Sónya too was busy all this time, but the aim of her efforts was quite different from Natásha's. She was putting away the things that had to be left behind and making a list of them as the countess wished, and she tried to get as much taken away with them as possible.

CHAPTER XVII

Before two o'clock in the afternoon the Rostóvs' four carriages, packed full and with the horses harnessed, stood at the front door. One by one the carts with the wounded had moved out of the yard.

The *calèche* in which Prince Andrew was being taken attracted Sónya's attention as it passed the front porch. With the help of a maid she was arranging a seat for the countess in the huge high coach that stood at the entrance.

"Whose *calèche* is that?" she inquired, leaning out of the carriage window.

"Why, didn't you know, Miss?" replied the maid. "The wounded prince: he spent the night in our house and is going with us."

"But who is it? What's his name?"

"It's our intended that was—Prince Bolkónski himself! They say he is dying," replied the maid with a sigh.

Sónya jumped out of the coach and ran to the countess. The countess, tired out and already dressed in shawl and bonnet for her journey, was pacing up and down the drawing room, waiting for the household to assemble for the usual silent prayer with closed doors before starting. Natásha was not in the room.

"Mamma," said Sónya, "Prince Andrew is here, mortally wounded. He is going with us."

The countess opened her eyes in dismay and, seizing Sónya's arm, glanced around.

"Natásha?" she murmured.

At that moment this news had only one significance for both of them. They knew their Natásha, and alarm as to what would happen if she heard this news stifled all sympathy for the man they both liked.

"Natásha does not know yet, but he is going with us," said Sónya.

"You say he is dying?"

Sónya nodded.

The countess put her arms around Sónya and began to cry.

"The ways of God are past finding out!" she thought, feeling that the Almighty Hand, hitherto unseen, was becoming manifest in all that was now taking place.

"Well, Mamma? Everything is ready. What's the matter?" asked Natásha, as with animated face she ran into the room.

"Nothing," answered the countess. "If everything is ready let us start."

And the countess bent over her reticule to hide her agitated face. Sónya embraced Natásha and kissed her.

Natásha looked at her inquiringly.

"What is it? What has happened?"

"Nothing... No..."

"Is it something very bad for me? What is it?" persisted Natásha with her quick intuition.

Sónya sighed and made no reply. The count, Pétya, Madame Schoss, MávraKuzmínichna, and Vasílich came into the drawing room and, having closed the doors, they all sat down and remained for some moments silently seated without looking at one another.

The count was the first to rise, and with a loud sigh crossed himself before the icon. All the others did the same. Then the count embraced MávraKuzmínichna and Vasílich, who were to remain in Moscow, and while they caught at his hand and kissed his shoulder he patted their backs lightly with some vaguely affectionate and comforting words. The countess went into the oratory and there Sónya found her on her knees before the icons that had been left here and there hanging on the wall. (The most precious ones, with which some family tradition was connected, were being taken with them.)

In the porch and in the yard the men whom Pétya had armed with swords and daggers, with trousers tucked inside their high boots and with belts and girdles tightened, were taking leave of those remaining behind.

As is always the case at a departure, much had been forgotten or put in the wrong place, and for a long time two menservants stood one on each side of the open door and the carriage steps waiting to help the countess in, while maids rushed with cushions and bundles from the house to the carriages, the *calèche*, the phaeton, and back again.

"They always will forget everything!" said the countess. "Don't you know I can't sit like that?"

And Dunyásha, with clenched teeth, without replying but with an aggrieved look on her face, hastily got into the coach to rearrange the seat.

"Oh, those servants!" said the count, swaying his head.

Efím, the old coachman, who was the only one the countess trusted to drive her, sat perched up high on the box and did not so much as glance round at what was going on behind him. From thirty years' experience he knew it would be some time yet before the order, "Be off, in God's name!" would be given him: and he knew that even when it was said he would be stopped once or twice more while they sent back to fetch something that had been forgotten, and even after that he would again be stopped and the countess herself would lean out of the window and beg him for the love of heaven to drive carefully down the hill. He knew all this and therefore waited calmly for what would happen, with more patience than the horses, especially the near one, the chestnut Falcon, who was pawing the ground and champing his bit. At last all were seated, the carriage steps were folded and pulled up, the door was shut, somebody was sent for a traveling case, and the countess leaned out and said what she had to say. Then Efím deliberately doffed his hat and began crossing himself. The postilion and all the other servants did the same. "Off, in God's name!" said Efím, putting on his hat. "Start!" The postilion started the horses, the off pole horse tugged at his collar, the high springs creaked, and the body of the coach swayed. The footman sprang onto the box of the moving coach which jolted as it passed out of the yard onto the uneven roadway; the other vehicles jolted in their turn, and the procession of carriages moved up the street. In the carriages, the *calèche*, and the phaeton, all crossed themselves as they passed the church opposite the house. Those who were to remain in Moscow walked on either side of the vehicles seeing the travelers off.

Rarely had Natásha experienced so joyful a feeling as now, sitting in the carriage beside the countess and gazing at the slowly receding walls of forsaken, agitated Moscow. Occasionally she leaned out of the carriage window and looked back and then forward at the long train of wounded in front of them. Almost at the head of the line she could see the raised hood of Prince Andrew's *calèche*. She did not know who was in it, but each time she looked at the procession her eyes sought that *calèche*. She knew it was right in front.

In Kúdrino, from the Nikítski, Présnya, and Podnovínsk Streets came several other trains of vehicles similar to the Rostóvs', and as they passed along the Sadóvaya Street the carriages and carts formed two rows abreast.

As they were going round the Súkharev water tower Natásha, who was inquisitively and alertly scrutinizing the people driving or walking past, suddenly cried out in joyful surprise:

"Dear me! Mamma, Sónya, look, it's he!"

"Who? Who?"

"Look! Yes, on my word, it's Bezúkhov!" said Natásha, putting her head out of the carriage and staring at a tall, stout man in a coachman's long coat, who from his manner of walking and moving was evidently a gentleman in disguise, and who was passing under the arch of the Súkharev tower accompanied by a small, sallow-faced, beardless old man in a frieze coat.

"Yes, it really is Bezúkhov in a coachman's coat, with a queer-looking old boy. Really," said Natásha, "look, look!"

"No, it's not he. How can you talk such nonsense?"

"Mamma," screamed Natásha, "I'll stake my head it's he! I assure you! Stop, stop!" she cried to the coachman.

But the coachman could not stop, for from the Meshchánski Street came more carts and carriages, and the Rostóvs were being shouted at to move on and not block the way.

In fact, however, though now much farther off than before, the Rostóvs all saw Pierre—or someone extraordinarily like him—in a coachman's coat, going down the street with head bent and a serious face beside a small, beardless old man who looked like a footman. That old man noticed a face thrust out of the carriage window gazing at them, and respectfully touching Pierre's elbow said something to him and pointed to the carriage. Pierre, evidently engrossed in thought, could not at first understand him. At length when he had understood and looked in the direction the old man indicated, he recognized Natásha, and following his first impulse stepped instantly and rapidly toward the coach. But having taken a dozen steps he seemed to remember something and stopped.

Natásha's face, leaning out of the window, beamed with quizzical kindliness.

"Peter Kirílovich, come here! We have recognized you! This is wonderful!" she cried, holding out her hand to him. "What are you doing? Why are you like this?"

Pierre took her outstretched hand and kissed it awkwardly as he walked along beside her while the coach still moved on.

"What is the matter, Count?" asked the countess in a surprised and commiserating tone.

"What? What? Why? Don't ask me," said Pierre, and looked round at Natásha whose radiant, happy expression—of which he was conscious without looking at her—filled him with enchantment.

"Are you remaining in Moscow, then?"

Pierre hesitated.

"In Moscow?" he said in a questioning tone. "Yes, in Moscow. Good-by!"

"Ah, if only I were a man! I'd certainly stay with you. How splendid!" said Natásha. "Mamma, if you'll let me, I'll stay!"

Pierre glanced absently at Natásha and was about to say something, but the countess interrupted him.

"You were at the battle, we heard."

"Yes, I was," Pierre answered. "There will be another battle tomorrow..." he began, but Natásha interrupted him.

"But what is the matter with you, Count? You are not like yourself...."

"Oh, don't ask me, don't ask me! I don't know myself. Tomorrow... But no! Good-by, good-by!" he muttered. "It's an awful time!" and dropping behind the carriage he stepped onto the pavement.

Natásha continued to lean out of the window for a long time, beaming at him with her kindly, slightly quizzical, happy smile.

CHAPTER XVIII

For the last two days, ever since leaving home, Pierre had been living in the empty house of his deceased benefactor, Bazdéev. This is how it happened.

When he woke up on the morning after his return to Moscow and his interview with Count Rostopchín, he could not for some time make out where he was and what was expected of him. When he was informed that among others awaiting him in his reception room there was a Frenchman who had brought a letter from his wife, the Countess Hélène, he felt suddenly overcome by that sense of confusion and hopelessness to which he was apt to succumb. He felt that everything was now at an end, all was in confusion and crumbling to pieces, that nobody was right or wrong, the future held nothing, and there was no escape from this position. Smiling unnaturally and muttering to himself, he first sat down on the sofa in an attitude of despair, then rose, went to the door of the reception room and peeped through the crack, returned flourishing his arms, and took up a book. His major-domo came in a second time to say that the Frenchman who had brought the letter from the countess was very anxious to see him if only for a minute, and that someone from Bazdéev's widow had called to ask Pierre to take charge of her husband's books, as she herself was leaving for the country.

"Oh, yes, in a minute; wait... or no! No, of course... go and say I will come directly," Pierre replied to the major-domo.

But as soon as the man had left the room Pierre took up his hat which was lying on the table and went out of his study by the other door. There was no one in the passage. He went along the whole length of this passage to the stairs and, frowning and rubbing his forehead with both hands, went down as far as the first landing. The hall porter was standing at the front door. From the landing where Pierre stood there was a second staircase leading to the back entrance. He went down that staircase and out into the yard. No one had seen him. But there were some carriages waiting, and as soon as Pierre stepped out of the gate the coachmen and the yard porter noticed him and raised their caps to him. When he felt he was being looked at he behaved like an ostrich which hides its head in a bush in order not to be seen: he hung his head and quickening his pace went down the street.

Of all the affairs awaiting Pierre that day the sorting of Joseph Bazdéev's books and papers appeared to him the most necessary.

He hired the first cab he met and told the driver to go to the Patriarch's Ponds, where the widow Bazdéev's house was.

Continually turning round to look at the rows of loaded carts that were making their way from all sides out of Moscow, and balancing his bulky body so as not to slip out of the ramshackle old vehicle, Pierre, experiencing the joyful feeling of a boy escaping from school, began to talk to his driver.

The man told him that arms were being distributed today at the Krémlin and that tomorrow everyone would be sent out beyond the Three Hills gates and a great battle would be fought there.

Having reached the Patriarch's Ponds Pierre found the Bazdéevs' house, where he had not been for a long time past. He went up to the gate. Gerásim, that sallow beardless old man Pierre had seen at Torzhók five years before with Joseph Bazdéev, came out in answer to his knock.

"At home?" asked Pierre.

"Owing to the present state of things Sophia Danílovna has gone to the Torzhók estate with the children, your excellency."

"I will come in all the same, I have to look through the books," said Pierre.

"Be so good as to step in. MakárAlexéevich, the brother of my late master—may the kingdom of heaven be his—has remained here, but he is in a weak state as you know," said the old servant.

Pierre knew that MakárAlexéevich was Joseph Bazdéev's half-insane brother and a hard drinker.

"Yes, yes, I know. Let us go in..." said Pierre and entered the house.

A tall, bald-headed old man with a red nose, wearing a dressing gown and with galoshes on his bare feet, stood in the anteroom. On seeing Pierre he muttered something angrily and went away along the passage.

"He was a very clever man but has now grown quite feeble, as your honor sees," said Gerásim. "Will you step into the study?" Pierre nodded. "As it was sealed up so it has remained, but Sophia Danílovna gave orders that if anyone should come from you they were to have the books."

Pierre went into that gloomy study which he had entered with such trepidation in his benefactor's lifetime. The room, dusty and untouched since the death of Joseph Bazdéev was now even gloomier.

Gerásim opened one of the shutters and left the room on tiptoe. Pierre went round the study, approached the cupboard in which the manuscripts were kept, and took out what had once been one of the most important, the holy of holies of the order. This was the authentic Scotch Acts with Bazdéev's notes and explanations. He sat down at the dusty writing table, and, having laid the manuscripts before him, opened them out, closed them, finally pushed them away, and resting his head on his hand sank into meditation.

Gerásim looked cautiously into the study several times and saw Pierre always sitting in the same attitude.

More than two hours passed and Gerásim took the liberty of making a slight noise at the door to attract his attention, but Pierre did not hear him.

"Is the cabman to be discharged, your honor?"

"Oh yes!" said Pierre, rousing himself and rising hurriedly. "Look here," he added, taking Gerásim by a button of his coat and looking down at the old man with moist, shining, and ecstatic eyes, "I say, do you know that there is going to be a battle tomorrow?"

"We heard so," replied the man.

"I beg you not to tell anyone who I am, and to do what I ask you."

"Yes, your excellency," replied Gerásim. "Will you have something to eat?"

War and Peace

"No, but I want something else. I want peasant clothes and a pistol," said Pierre, unexpectedly blushing.

"Yes, your excellency," said Gerásim after thinking for a moment.

All the rest of that day Pierre spent alone in his benefactor's study, and Gerásim heard him pacing restlessly from one corner to another and talking to himself. And he spent the night on a bed made up for him there.

Gerásim, being a servant who in his time had seen many strange things, accepted Pierre's taking up his residence in the house without surprise, and seemed pleased to have someone to wait on. That same evening—without even asking himself what they were wanted for— he procured a coachman's coat and cap for Pierre, and promised to get him the pistol next day. MakárAlexéevich came twice that evening shuffling along in his galoshes as far as the door and stopped and looked ingratiatingly at Pierre. But as soon as Pierre turned toward him he wrapped his dressing gown around him with a shamefaced and angry look and hurried away. It was when Pierre (wearing the coachman's coat which Gerásim had procured for him and had disinfected by steam) was on his way with the old man to buy the pistol at the Súkharev market that he met the Rostóvs.

CHAPTER XIX

K utúzov's order to retreat through Moscow to the Ryazán road was issued at night on the first of September.

The first troops started at once, and during the night they marched slowly and steadily without hurry. At daybreak, however, those nearing the town at the Dorogomílov bridge saw ahead of them masses of soldiers crowding and hurrying across the bridge, ascending on the opposite side and blocking the streets and alleys, while endless masses of troops were bearing down on them from behind, and an unreasoning hurry and alarm overcame them. They all rushed forward to the bridge, onto it, and to the fords and the boats. Kutúzov himself had driven round by side streets to the other side of Moscow.

By ten o'clock in the morning of the second of September, only the rear guard remained in the Dorogomílov suburb, where they had ample room. The main army was on the other side of Moscow or beyond it.

At that very time, at ten in the morning of the second of September, Napoleon was standing among his troops on the Poklónny Hill looking at the panorama spread out before him. From the twenty-sixth of August to the second of September, that is from the battle of Borodinó to the entry of the French into Moscow, during the whole of that agitating, memorable week, there had been the extraordinary autumn weather that always comes as a surprise, when the sun hangs low and gives more heat than in spring, when everything shines so brightly in the rare clear atmosphere that the eyes smart, when the lungs are strengthened and refreshed by inhaling the aromatic autumn air, when even the nights are warm, and when in those dark warm nights, golden stars startle and delight us continually by falling from the sky.

At ten in the morning of the second of September this weather still held.

The brightness of the morning was magical. Moscow seen from the Poklónny Hill lay spaciously spread out with her river, her gardens, and her churches, and she seemed to be living her usual life, her cupolas glittering like stars in the sunlight.

The view of the strange city with its peculiar architecture, such as he had never seen before, filled Napoleon with the rather envious and uneasy curiosity men feel when they see an alien form of life that has no knowledge of them. This city was evidently living with the full force of its own life. By the indefinite signs which, even at a distance, distinguish a living body from a dead one, Napoleon from the Poklónny Hill perceived the throb of life in the town and felt, as it were, the breathing of that great and beautiful body.

Every Russian looking at Moscow feels her to be a mother; every foreigner who sees her, even if ignorant of her significance as the mother city, must feel her feminine character, and Napoleon felt it.

"Cettevilleasiatique aux innombrableséglises, Moscou la sainte. La voilà doncenfin, cettefameuseville! Il était temps," * said he, and dismounting he ordered a plan of Moscow to be spread out before him, and summoned Lelorgned'Ideville, the interpreter.

* "That Asiatic city of the innumerable churches, holy Moscow! Here it is then at last, that famous city. It was high time."

"A town captured by the enemy is like a maid who has lost her honor," thought he (he had said so to Túchkov at Smolénsk). From that point of view he gazed at the Oriental beauty he had not seen before. It seemed strange to him that his long-felt wish, which had seemed unattainable, had at last been realized. In the clear morning light he gazed now at the city and now at the plan, considering its details, and the assurance of possessing it agitated and awed him.

"But could it be otherwise?" he thought. "Here is this capital at my feet. Where is Alexander now, and of what is he thinking? A strange, beautiful, and majestic city; and a strange and majestic moment! In what light must I appear to them!" thought he, thinking of his troops. "Here she is, the reward for all those fainthearted men," he reflected, glancing at those near him and at the troops who were approaching and forming up. "One word from me, one movement of my hand, and that ancient capital of the Tsars would perish. But my clemency is always ready to descend upon the vanquished. I must be magnanimous and truly great. But no, it can't be true that I am in Moscow," he suddenly thought. "Yet here she is lying at my feet, with her golden domes and crosses scintillating and twinkling in the sunshine. But I shall spare her. On the ancient monuments of barbarism and despotism I will inscribe great words of justice and mercy.... It is just this which Alexander will feel most painfully, I know him." (It seemed to Napoleon that the chief import of what was taking place lay in the personal struggle between himself and Alexander.) "From the height of the Krémlin—yes, there is the Krémlin, yes—I will give them just laws; I will teach them the meaning of true civilization, I will make generations of boyars remember their conqueror with love. I will tell the deputation that I did not, and do not, desire war, that I have waged war only against the false policy of their court; that I love and respect Alexander and that in Moscow I will accept terms of peace worthy of myself and of my people. I do not wish to utilize the fortunes of war to humiliate an honored monarch. 'Boyars,' I will say to them, 'I do not desire war, I desire the peace and welfare of all my subjects.' However, I know their presence will inspire me, and I shall speak to them as I always do: clearly, impressively, and majestically. But can it be true that I am in Moscow? Yes, there she lies."

"Qu'onm'amène les boyars," * said he to his suite.

* "Bring the boyars to me."

A general with a brilliant suite galloped off at once to fetch the boyars.

Two hours passed. Napoleon had lunched and was again standing in the same place on the Poklónny Hill awaiting the deputation. His speech to the boyars had already taken definite shape in his imagination. That speech was full of dignity and greatness as Napoleon understood it.

He was himself carried away by the tone of magnanimity he intended to adopt toward Moscow. In his imagination he appointed days for assemblies at the palace of the Tsars, at which Russian notables and his own would mingle. He mentally appointed a governor, one who would win the hearts of the people. Having learned that there were many charitable institutions in Moscow he mentally decided that he would shower favors on them all. He thought that, as in Africa he had to put on a burnoose and sit in a mosque, so in Moscow he must be beneficent like the Tsars. And in order finally to touch the hearts of the Russians—and being like all Frenchmen unable to imagine anything sentimental without a reference to *ma chère, ma tendre, ma pauvremère* * —he decided that he would place an inscription on all these establishments in large letters: "This establishment is dedicated to my dear mother." Or no, it should be simply: *Maison de ma Mère*, *(2) he concluded. "But am I really in Moscow? Yes, here it lies before me, but why is the deputation from the city so long in appearing?" he wondered.

* "My dear, my tender, my poor mother."

* (2) "House of my Mother."

Meanwhile an agitated consultation was being carried on in whispers among his generals and marshals at the rear of his suite. Those sent to fetch the deputation had returned with the news that Moscow was empty, that everyone had left it. The faces of those who were not conferring together were pale and perturbed. They were not alarmed by the fact that Moscow had been abandoned by its inhabitants (grave as that fact seemed), but by the question how to tell the Emperor—without putting him in the terrible position of appearing ridiculous—that he had been awaiting the boyars so long in vain: that there were drunken mobs left in Moscow but no one else. Some said that a deputation of some sort must be scraped together, others disputed that opinion and maintained that the Emperor should first be carefully and skillfully prepared, and then told the truth.

"He will have to be told, all the same," said some gentlemen of the suite. "But, gentlemen..."

The position was the more awkward because the Emperor, meditating upon his magnanimous plans, was pacing patiently up and down before the outspread map, occasionally glancing along the road to Moscow from under his lifted hand with a bright and proud smile.

"But it's impossible…" declared the gentlemen of the suite, shrugging their shoulders but not venturing to utter the implied word—*le ridicule*….

At last the Emperor, tired of futile expectation, his actor's instinct suggesting to him that the sublime moment having been too long drawn out was beginning to lose its sublimity, gave a sign with his hand. A single report of a signaling gun followed, and the troops, who were already spread out on different sides of Moscow, moved into the city through the Tver, Kalúga, and Dorogomílov gates. Faster and faster, vying with one another, they moved at the double or at a trot, vanishing amid the clouds of dust they raised and making the air ring with a deafening roar of mingling shouts.

Drawn on by the movement of his troops Napoleon rode with them as far as the Dorogomílov gate, but there again stopped and, dismounting from his horse, paced for a long time by the Kámmer-Kollézski rampart, awaiting the deputation.

CHAPTER XX

Meanwhile Moscow was empty. There were still people in it, perhaps a fiftieth part of its former inhabitants had remained, but it was empty. It was empty in the sense that a dying queenless hive is empty.

In a queenless hive no life is left though to a superficial glance it seems as much alive as other hives.

The bees circle round a queenless hive in the hot beams of the midday sun as gaily as around the living hives; from a distance it smells of honey like the others, and bees fly in and out in the same way. But one has only to observe that hive to realize that there is no longer any life in it. The bees do not fly in the same way, the smell and the sound that meet the beekeeper are not the same. To the beekeeper's tap on the wall of the sick hive, instead of the former instant unanimous humming of tens of thousands of bees with their abdomens threateningly compressed, and producing by the rapid vibration of their wings an aerial living sound, the only reply is a disconnected buzzing from different parts of the deserted hive. From the alighting board, instead of the former spirituous fragrant smell of honey and venom, and the warm whiffs of crowded life, comes an odor of emptiness and decay mingling with the smell of honey. There are no longer sentinels sounding the alarm with their abdomens raised, and ready to die in defense of the hive. There is no longer the measured quiet sound of throbbing activity, like the sound of boiling water, but diverse discordant sounds of disorder. In and out of the hive long black robber bees smeared with honey fly timidly and shiftily. They do not sting, but crawl away from danger.

Formerly only bees laden with honey flew into the hive, and they flew out empty; now they fly out laden. The beekeeper opens the lower part of the hive and peers in. Instead of black, glossy bees—tamed by toil, clinging to one another's legs and drawing out the wax, with a ceaseless hum of labor—that used to hang in long clusters down to the floor of the hive, drowsy shriveled bees crawl about separately in various directions on the floor and walls of the hive. Instead of a neatly glued floor, swept by the bees with the fanning of their wings, there is a floor littered with bits of wax, excrement, dying bees scarcely moving their legs, and dead ones that have not been cleared away.

The beekeeper opens the upper part of the hive and examines the super. Instead of serried rows of bees sealing up every gap in the combs and keeping the brood warm, he sees the skillful complex structures of the combs, but no longer in their former state of purity. All is neglected and foul. Black robber bees are swiftly and stealthily prowling about the combs, and the short home bees, shriveled and listless as if they were old, creep slowly about without trying to hinder the robbers, having lost all motive and all sense of life. Drones, bumblebees, wasps, and butterflies knock awkwardly against the walls of the hive in their flight. Here and there among the cells containing dead brood and honey an angry buzzing can sometimes be heard. Here and there a couple of bees, by force of habit and custom cleaning out the brood cells, with efforts beyond their strength laboriously drag away a dead bee or bumblebee without knowing why they do it. In another corner two old bees are languidly fighting, or cleaning themselves, or feeding one another, without themselves knowing whether they do it with friendly or hostile intent. In a third place a crowd of bees, crushing one another, attack some victim and fight and smother it, and the victim, enfeebled or killed, drops from above slowly and lightly as a feather, among the heap of corpses. The keeper opens the two center partitions to examine the brood cells. In place of the former close dark circles formed by thousands of bees sitting back to back and guarding the high mystery of generation, he sees hundreds of dull, listless, and sleepy shells of bees. They have almost all died unawares, sitting in the sanctuary they had guarded and which is now no more. They reek of decay and death. Only a few of them still move, rise, and feebly fly to settle on the enemy's hand, lacking the spirit to die stinging him; the rest are dead and fall as lightly as fish scales. The beekeeper closes the hive, chalks a mark on it, and when he has time tears out its contents and burns it clean.

So in the same way Moscow was empty when Napoleon, weary, uneasy, and morose, paced up and down in front of the Kámmer-Kollézski rampart, awaiting what to his mind was a necessary, if but formal, observance of the proprieties—a deputation.

In various corners of Moscow there still remained a few people aimlessly moving about, following their old habits and hardly aware of what they were doing.

When with due circumspection Napoleon was informed that Moscow was empty, he looked angrily at his informant, turned away, and silently continued to walk to and fro.

"My carriage!" he said.

He took his seat beside the aide-de-camp on duty and drove into the suburb. "Moscow deserted!" he said to himself. "What an incredible event!"

He did not drive into the town, but put up at an inn in the Dorogomílov suburb.

The *coup de théâtre* had not come off.

CHAPTER XXI

The Russian troops were passing through Moscow from two o'clock at night till two in the afternoon and bore away with them the wounded and the last of the inhabitants who were leaving.

The greatest crush during the movement of the troops took place at the Stone, Moskvá, and Yaúza bridges.

While the troops, dividing into two parts when passing around the Krémlin, were thronging the Moskvá and the Stone bridges, a great many soldiers, taking advantage of the stoppage and congestion, turned back from the bridges and slipped stealthily and silently past the church of Vasíli the Beatified and under the Borovítski gate, back up the hill to the Red Square where some instinct told them they could easily take things not belonging to them. Crowds of the kind seen at cheap sales filled all the passages and alleys of the Bazaar. But there were no dealers with voices of ingratiating affability inviting customers to enter; there were no hawkers, nor the usual motley crowd of female purchasers—but only soldiers, in uniforms and overcoats though without muskets, entering the Bazaar empty-handed and silently making their way out through its passages with bundles. Tradesmen and their assistants (of whom there were but few) moved about among the soldiers quite bewildered. They unlocked their shops and locked them up again, and themselves carried goods away with the help of their assistants. On the square in front of the Bazaar were drummers beating the muster call. But the roll of the drums did not make the looting soldiers run in the direction of the drum as formerly, but made them, on the contrary, run farther away. Among the soldiers in the shops and passages some men were to be seen in gray coats, with closely shaven heads. Two officers, one with a scarf over his uniform and mounted on a lean, dark-gray horse, the other in an overcoat and on foot, stood at the corner of Ilyínka Street, talking. A third officer galloped up to them.

"The general orders them all to be driven out at once, without fail. This is outrageous! Half the men have dispersed."

"Where are you off to?... Where?..." he shouted to three infantrymen without muskets who, holding up the skirts of their overcoats, were slipping past him into the Bazaar passage. "Stop, you rascals!"

"But how are you going to stop them?" replied another officer. "There is no getting them together. The army should push on before the rest bolt, that's all!"

"How can one push on? They are stuck there, wedged on the bridge, and don't move. Shouldn't we put a cordon round to prevent the rest from running away?"

"Come, go in there and drive them out!" shouted the senior officer.

The officer in the scarf dismounted, called up a drummer, and went with him into the arcade. Some soldiers started running away in a group. A shopkeeper with red pimples on his cheeks near the nose, and a calm, persistent, calculating expression on his plump face, hurriedly and ostentatiously approached the officer, swinging his arms.

"Your honor!" said he. "Be so good as to protect us! We won't grudge trifles, you are welcome to anything—we shall be delighted! Pray!... I'll fetch a piece of cloth at once for such an honorable gentleman, or even two pieces with pleasure. For we feel how it is; but what's all this—sheer robbery! If you please, could not guards be placed if only to let us close the shop...."

Several shopkeepers crowded round the officer.

"Eh, what twaddle!" said one of them, a thin, stern-looking man. "When one's head is gone one doesn't weep for one's hair! Take what any of you like!" And flourishing his arm energetically he turned sideways to the officer.

"It's all very well for you, Iván Sidórych, to talk," said the first tradesman angrily. "Please step inside, your honor!"

"Talk indeed!" cried the thin one. "In my three shops here I have a hundred thousand rubles' worth of goods. Can they be saved when the army has gone? Eh, what people! 'Against God's might our hands can't fight.'"

"Come inside, your honor!" repeated the tradesman, bowing.

The officer stood perplexed and his face showed indecision.

"It's not my business!" he exclaimed, and strode on quickly down one of the passages.

From one open shop came the sound of blows and vituperation, and just as the officer came up to it a man in a gray coat with a shaven head was flung out violently.

This man, bent double, rushed past the tradesman and the officer. The officer pounced on the soldiers who were in the shops, but at that moment fearful screams reached them from the huge crowd on the Moskvá bridge and the officer ran out into the square.

"What is it? What is it?" he asked, but his comrade was already galloping off past Vasíli the Beatified in the direction from which the screams came.

The officer mounted his horse and rode after him. When he reached the bridge he saw two unlimbered guns, the infantry crossing the bridge, several overturned carts, and frightened and laughing faces among the troops. Beside the cannon a cart was standing to which two horses were harnessed. Four borzois with collars were pressing close to the wheels. The cart was loaded high, and at the very top, beside a child's chair with its legs in the air, sat a peasant woman uttering piercing and desperate shrieks. He was told by his fellow officers that the screams of the crowd and the shrieks of the woman were due to the fact that General Ermólov, coming up to the crowd and learning that soldiers were dispersing among the shops while crowds of civilians blocked the bridge, had ordered two guns to be unlimbered and made a show of firing at the bridge. The crowd, crushing one another, upsetting carts, and shouting and squeezing desperately, had cleared off the bridge and the troops were now moving forward.

CHAPTER XXII

Meanwhile, the city itself was deserted. There was hardly anyone in the streets. The gates and shops were all closed, only here and there round the taverns solitary shouts or drunken songs could be heard. Nobody drove through the streets and footsteps were rarely heard. The Povarskáya was quite still and deserted. The huge courtyard of the Rostóvs' house was littered with wisps of hay and with dung from the horses, and not a soul was to be seen there. In the great drawing room of the house, which had been left with all it contained, were two people. They were the yard porter Ignát, and the page boy Míshka, Vasílich's grandson who had stayed in Moscow with his grandfather. Míshka had opened the clavichord and was strumming on it with one finger. The yard porter, his arms akimbo, stood smiling with satisfaction before the large mirror.

"Isn't it fine, eh, Uncle Ignát?" said the boy, suddenly beginning to strike the keyboard with both hands.

"Only fancy!" answered Ignát, surprised at the broadening grin on his face in the mirror.

"Impudence! Impudence!" they heard behind them the voice of MávraKuzmínichna who had entered silently. "How he's grinning, the fat mug! Is that what you're here for? Nothing's cleared away down there and Vasílich is worn out. Just you wait a bit!"

Ignát left off smiling, adjusted his belt, and went out of the room with meekly downcast eyes.

"Aunt, I did it gently," said the boy.

"I'll give you something gently, you monkey you!" cried MávraKuzmínichna, raising her arm threateningly. "Go and get the samovar to boil for your grandfather."

MávraKuzmínichna flicked the dust off the clavichord and closed it, and with a deep sigh left the drawing room and locked its main door.

Going out into the yard she paused to consider where she should go next—to drink tea in the servants' wing with Vasílich, or into the storeroom to put away what still lay about.

She heard the sound of quick footsteps in the quiet street. Someone stopped at the gate, and the latch rattled as someone tried to open it. MávraKuzmínichna went to the gate.

"Who do you want?"

"The count—Count IlyáAndréevichRostóv."

"And who are you?"

"An officer, I have to see him," came the reply in a pleasant, well-bred Russian voice.

MávraKuzmínichna opened the gate and an officer of eighteen, with the round face of a Rostóv, entered the yard.

"They have gone away, sir. Went away yesterday at vespertime," said MávraKuzmínichna cordially.

The young officer standing in the gateway, as if hesitating whether to enter or not, clicked his tongue.

"Ah, how annoying!" he muttered. "I should have come yesterday.... Ah, what a pity."

Meanwhile, MávraKuzmínichna was attentively and sympathetically examining the familiar Rostóv features of the young man's face, his tattered coat and trodden-down boots.

"What did you want to see the count for?" she asked.

"Oh well... it can't be helped!" said he in a tone of vexation and placed his hand on the gate as if to leave.

He again paused in indecision.

"You see," he suddenly said, "I am a kinsman of the count's and he has been very kind to me. As you see" (he glanced with an amused air and good-natured smile at his coat and boots) "my things are worn out and I have no money, so I was going to ask the count..."

MávraKuzmínichna did not let him finish.

"Just wait a minute, sir. One little moment," said she.

And as soon as the officer let go of the gate handle she turned and, hurrying away on her old legs, went through the back yard to the servants' quarters.

While MávraKuzmínichna was running to her room the officer walked about the yard gazing at his worn-out boots with lowered head and a faint smile on his lips. "What a pity I've missed Uncle! What a nice old woman! Where has she run off to? And how am I to find the nearest way to overtake my regiment, which must by now be getting near the Rogózhski gate?" thought he. Just then MávraKuzmínichna appeared from behind the corner of the house with a frightened yet resolute look, carrying a rolled-up check kerchief in her hand. While still a few steps from the officer she unfolded the kerchief and took out of it a white twenty-five-ruble assignat and hastily handed it to him.

"If his excellency had been at home, as a kinsman he would of course... but as it is..."

MávraKuzmínichna grew abashed and confused. The officer did not decline, but took the note quietly and thanked her.

"If the count had been at home..." MávraKuzmínichna went on apologetically. "Christ be with you, sir! May God preserve you!" said she, bowing as she saw him out.

Swaying his head and smiling as if amused at himself, the officer ran almost at a trot through the deserted streets toward the Yaúza bridge to overtake his regiment.

But MávraKuzmínichna stood at the closed gate for some time with moist eyes, pensively swaying her head and feeling an unexpected flow of motherly tenderness and pity for the unknown young officer.

CHAPTER XXIII

From an unfinished house on the Varvárka, the ground floor of which was a dramshop, came drunken shouts and songs. On benches round the tables in a dirty little room sat some ten factory hands. Tipsy and perspiring, with dim eyes and wide-open mouths, they were all laboriously singing some song or other. They were singing discordantly, arduously, and with great effort, evidently not because they wished to sing, but because they wanted to show they were drunk and on a spree. One, a tall, fair-haired lad in a clean blue coat, was standing over the others. His face with its fine straight nose would have been handsome had it not been for his thin, compressed, twitching lips and dull, gloomy, fixed eyes. Evidently possessed by some idea, he stood over those who were singing, and solemnly and jerkily flourished above their heads his white arm with the sleeve turned up to the elbow, trying unnaturally to spread out his dirty fingers. The sleeve of his coat kept slipping down and he always carefully rolled it up again with his left hand, as if it were most important that the sinewy white arm he was flourishing should be bare. In the midst of the song cries were heard, and fighting and blows in the passage and porch. The tall lad waved his arm.

"Stop it!" he exclaimed peremptorily. "There's a fight, lads!" And, still rolling up his sleeve, he went out to the porch.

The factory hands followed him. These men, who under the leadership of the tall lad were drinking in the dramshop that morning, had brought the publican some skins from the factory and for this had had drink served them. The blacksmiths from a neighboring smithy, hearing the sounds of revelry in the tavern and supposing it to have been broken into, wished to force their way in too and a fight in the porch had resulted.

The publican was fighting one of the smiths at the door, and when the workmen came out the smith, wrenching himself free from the tavern keeper, fell face downward on the pavement.

Another smith tried to enter the doorway, pressing against the publican with his chest.

The lad with the turned-up sleeve gave the smith a blow in the face and cried wildly: "They're fighting us, lads!"

At that moment the first smith got up and, scratching his bruised face to make it bleed, shouted in a tearful voice: "Police! Murder!... They've killed a man, lads!"

"Oh, gracious me, a man beaten to death—killed!..." screamed a woman coming out of a gate close by.

A crowd gathered round the bloodstained smith.

"Haven't you robbed people enough—taking their last shirts?" said a voice addressing the publican. "What have you killed a man for, you thief?"

The tall lad, standing in the porch, turned his bleared eyes from the publican to the smith and back again as if considering whom he ought to fight now.

"Murderer!" he shouted suddenly to the publican. "Bind him, lads!"

"I daresay you would like to bind me!" shouted the publican, pushing away the men advancing on him, and snatching his cap from his head he flung it on the ground.

As if this action had some mysterious and menacing significance, the workmen surrounding the publican paused in indecision.

"I know the law very well, mates! I'll take the matter to the captain of police. You think I won't get to him? Robbery is not permitted to anybody nowadays!" shouted the publican, picking up his cap.

"Come along then! Come along then!" the publican and the tall young fellow repeated one after the other, and they moved up the street together.

The bloodstained smith went beside them. The factory hands and others followed behind, talking and shouting.

At the corner of the Moroséyka, opposite a large house with closed shutters and bearing a bootmaker's signboard, stood a score of thin, worn-out, gloomy-faced bootmakers, wearing overalls and long tattered coats.

"He should pay folks off properly," a thin workingman, with frowning brows and a straggly beard, was saying.

"But he's sucked our blood and now he thinks he's quit of us. He's been misleading us all the week and now that he's brought us to this pass he's made off."

On seeing the crowd and the bloodstained man the workman ceased speaking, and with eager curiosity all the bootmakers joined the moving crowd.

"Where are all the folks going?"

"Why, to the police, of course!"

"I say, is it true that we have been beaten?" "And what did you think? Look what folks are saying."

Questions and answers were heard. The publican, taking advantage of the increased crowd, dropped behind and returned to his tavern.

The tall youth, not noticing the disappearance of his foe, waved his bare arm and went on talking incessantly, attracting general attention to himself. It was around him that the people chiefly crowded, expecting answers from him to the questions that occupied all their minds.

"He must keep order, keep the law, that's what the government is there for. Am I not right, good Christians?" said the tall youth, with a scarcely perceptible smile. "He thinks there's no government! How can one do without government? Or else there would be plenty who'd rob us."

"Why talk nonsense?" rejoined voices in the crowd. "Will they give up Moscow like this? They told you that for fun, and you believed it! Aren't there plenty of troops on the march? Let *him* in, indeed! That's what the government is for. You'd better listen to what people are saying," said some of the mob pointing to the tall youth.

By the wall of China-Town a smaller group of people were gathered round a man in a frieze coat who held a paper in his hand.

"An ukáse, they are reading an ukáse! Reading an ukáse!" cried voices in the crowd, and the people rushed toward the reader.

The man in the frieze coat was reading the broadsheet of August 31. When the crowd collected round him he seemed confused, but at the demand of the tall lad who had pushed his way up to him, he began in a rather tremulous voice to read the sheet from the beginning.

"Early tomorrow I shall go to his Serene Highness," he read (*"Sirin Highness,"* said the tall fellow with a triumphant smile on his lips and a frown on his brow), "to consult with him to act, and to aid the army to exterminate these scoundrels. We too will take part..." the reader went on, and then paused ("Do you see," shouted the youth victoriously, "he's going to clear up the whole affair for you...."), "in destroying them, and will send these visitors to the devil. I will come back to dinner, and we'll set to work. We will do, completely do, and undo these scoundrels."

The last words were read out in the midst of complete silence. The tall lad hung his head gloomily. It was evident that no one had understood the last part. In particular, the words "I will come back to dinner," evidently displeased both reader and audience. The people's minds were tuned to a high pitch and this was too simple and needlessly comprehensible—it was what any one of them might have said and therefore was what an ukáse emanating from the highest authority should not say.

They all stood despondent and silent. The tall youth moved his lips and swayed from side to side.

"We should ask him... that's he himself?"... "Yes, ask him indeed!... Why not? He'll explain"... voices in the rear of the crowd were suddenly heard saying, and the general attention turned to the police superintendent's trap which drove into the square attended by two mounted dragoons.

The superintendent of police, who had gone that morning by Count Rostopchín's orders to burn the barges and had in connection with that matter acquired a large sum of money which was at that moment in his pocket, on seeing a crowd bearing down upon him told his coachman to stop.

"What people are these?" he shouted to the men, who were moving singly and timidly in the direction of his trap.

"What people are these?" he shouted again, receiving no answer.

"Your honor..." replied the shopman in the frieze coat, "your honor, in accord with the proclamation of his highest excellency the count, they desire to serve, not sparing their lives, and it is not any kind of riot, but as his highest excellence said..."

"The count has not left, he is here, and an order will be issued concerning you," said the superintendent of police. "Go on!" he ordered his coachman.

The crowd halted, pressing around those who had heard what the superintendent had said, and looking at the departing trap.

The superintendent of police turned round at that moment with a scared look, said something to his coachman, and his horses increased their speed.

"It's a fraud, lads! Lead the way to him, himself!" shouted the tall youth. "Don't let him go, lads! Let him answer us! Keep him!" shouted different people and the people dashed in pursuit of the trap.

Following the superintendent of police and talking loudly the crowd went in the direction of the Lubyánka Street.

"There now, the gentry and merchants have gone away and left us to perish. Do they think we're dogs?" voices in the crowd were heard saying more and more frequently.

CHAPTER XXIV

O n the evening of the first of September, after his interview with
Kutúzov, Count Rostopchín had returned to Moscow mortified
and offended because he had not been invited to attend the council of
war, and because Kutúzov had paid no attention to his offer to take part
in the defense of the city; amazed also at the novel outlook revealed
to him at the camp, which treated the tranquillity of the capital and
its patriotic fervor as not merely secondary but quite irrelevant and
unimportant matters. Distressed, offended, and surprised by all this,
Rostopchín had returned to Moscow. After supper he lay down on a
sofa without undressing, and was awakened soon after midnight by a
courier bringing him a letter from Kutúzov. This letter requested the
count to send police officers to guide the troops through the town,
as the army was retreating to the Ryazán road beyond Moscow. This
was not news to Rostopchín. He had known that Moscow would be
abandoned not merely since his interview the previous day with
Kutúzov on the Poklónny Hill but ever since the battle of Borodinó,
for all the generals who came to Moscow after that battle had said
unanimously that it was impossible to fight another battle, and
since then the government property had been removed every night,
and half the inhabitants had left the city with Rostopchín's own
permission. Yet all the same this information astonished and irritated
the count, coming as it did in the form of a simple note with an order
from Kutúzov, and received at night, breaking in on his beauty sleep.

When later on in his memoirs Count Rostopchín explained his
actions at this time, he repeatedly says that he was then actuated by
two important considerations: to maintain tranquillity in Moscow
and expedite the departure of the inhabitants. If one accepts this

twofold aim all Rostopchín's actions appear irreproachable. "Why were the holy relics, the arms, ammunition, gunpowder, and stores of corn not removed? Why were thousands of inhabitants deceived into believing that Moscow would not be given up—and thereby ruined?" "To preserve the tranquillity of the city," explains Count Rostopchín. "Why were bundles of useless papers from the government offices, and Leppich's balloon and other articles removed?" "To leave the town empty," explains Count Rostopchín. One need only admit that public tranquillity is in danger and any action finds a justification.

All the horrors of the reign of terror were based only on solicitude for public tranquillity.

On what, then, was Count Rostopchín's fear for the tranquillity of Moscow based in 1812? What reason was there for assuming any probability of an uprising in the city? The inhabitants were leaving it and the retreating troops were filling it. Why should that cause the masses to riot?

Neither in Moscow nor anywhere in Russia did anything resembling an insurrection ever occur when the enemy entered a town. More than ten thousand people were still in Moscow on the first and second of September, and except for a mob in the governor's courtyard, assembled there at his bidding, nothing happened. It is obvious that there would have been even less reason to expect a disturbance among the people if after the battle of Borodinó, when the surrender of Moscow became certain or at least probable, Rostopchín instead of exciting the people by distributing arms and broadsheets had taken steps to remove all the holy relics, the gunpowder, munitions, and money, and had told the population plainly that the town would be abandoned.

Rostopchín, though he had patriotic sentiments, was a sanguine and impulsive man who had always moved in the highest administrative circles and had no understanding at all of the people he supposed himself to be guiding. Ever since the enemy's entry into Smolénsk he had in imagination been playing the role of director of the popular feeling of "the heart of Russia." Not only did it seem to him (as to all administrators) that he controlled the external actions of Moscow's inhabitants, but he also thought he controlled their mental attitude by means of his broadsheets and posters, written in a coarse tone which the people despise in their own class and do not understand from those in authority. Rostopchín was so pleased with the fine role of leader of popular feeling, and had grown so used to it, that the necessity of relinquishing that role and abandoning Moscow without any heroic display took him unawares and he suddenly felt the ground slip away from under his feet, so that he positively did not know what to do. Though he knew it was coming, he did not till the last moment wholeheartedly believe that Moscow would be abandoned, and did not prepare for it. The inhabitants left against his wishes. If the government offices were removed, this was only done on the demand of officials to whom the count yielded reluctantly. He was absorbed in the role he had created for himself. As is often the case with those gifted with an ardent imagination, though he had long known that Moscow would be abandoned he knew it only with his intellect, he did not believe it in his heart and did not adapt himself mentally to this new position of affairs.

All his painstaking and energetic activity (in how far it was useful and had any effect on the people is another question) had been simply directed toward arousing in the masses his own feeling of patriotic hatred of the French.

But when events assumed their true historical character, when expressing hatred for the French in words proved insufficient, when it was not even possible to express that hatred by fighting a battle, when self-confidence was of no avail in relation to the one question before Moscow, when the whole population streamed out of Moscow as one man, abandoning their belongings and proving by that negative action all the depth of their national feeling, then the role chosen by Rostopchín suddenly appeared senseless. He unexpectedly felt himself ridiculous, weak, and alone, with no ground to stand on.

When, awakened from his sleep, he received that cold, peremptory note from Kutúzov, he felt the more irritated the more he felt himself to blame. All that he had been specially put in charge of, the state property which he should have removed, was still in Moscow and it was no longer possible to take the whole of it away.

"Who is to blame for it? Who has let things come to such a pass?" he ruminated. "Not I, of course. I had everything ready. I had Moscow firmly in hand. And this is what they have let it come to! Villains! Traitors!" he thought, without clearly defining who the villains and traitors were, but feeling it necessary to hate those traitors whoever they might be who were to blame for the false and ridiculous position in which he found himself.

All that night Count Rostopchín issued orders, for which people came to him from all parts of Moscow. Those about him had never seen the count so morose and irritable.

"Your excellency, the Director of the Registrar's Department has sent for instructions.... From the Consistory, from the Senate, from the University, from the Foundling Hospital, the Suffragan has sent... asking for information.... What are your orders about the Fire Brigade? From the governor of the prison... from the superintendent of the lunatic asylum..." All night long such announcements were continually being received by the count.

To all these inquiries he gave brief and angry replies indicating that orders from him were not now needed, that the whole affair, carefully prepared by him, had now been ruined by somebody, and that that somebody would have to bear the whole responsibility for all that might happen.

"Oh, tell that blockhead," he said in reply to the question from the Registrar's Department, "that he should remain to guard his documents. Now why are you asking silly questions about the Fire Brigade? They have horses, let them be off to Vladímir, and not leave them to the French."

"Your excellency, the superintendent of the lunatic asylum has come: what are your commands?"

"My commands? Let them go away, that's all.... And let the lunatics out into the town. When lunatics command our armies God evidently means these other madmen to be free."

In reply to an inquiry about the convicts in the prison, Count Rostopchín shouted angrily at the governor:

"Do you expect me to give you two battalions—which we have not got—for a convoy? Release them, that's all about it!"

"Your excellency, there are some political prisoners, Meshkóv, Vereshchágin..."

"Vereshchágin! Hasn't he been hanged yet?" shouted Rostopchín. "Bring him to me!"

CHAPTER XXV

Toward nine o'clock in the morning, when the troops were already moving through Moscow, nobody came to the count any more for instructions. Those who were able to get away were going of their own accord, those who remained behind decided for themselves what they must do.

The count ordered his carriage that he might drive to Sokólniki, and sat in his study with folded hands, morose, sallow, and taciturn.

In quiet and untroubled times it seems to every administrator that it is only by his efforts that the whole population under his rule is kept going, and in this consciousness of being indispensable every administrator finds the chief reward of his labor and efforts. While the sea of history remains calm the ruler-administrator in his frail bark, holding on with a boat hook to the ship of the people and himself moving, naturally imagines that his efforts move the ship he is holding on to. But as soon as a storm arises and the sea begins to heave and the ship to move, such a delusion is no longer possible. The ship moves independently with its own enormous motion, the boat hook no longer reaches the moving vessel, and suddenly the administrator, instead of appearing a ruler and a source of power, becomes an insignificant, useless, feeble man.

Rostopchín felt this, and it was this which exasperated him.

The superintendent of police, whom the crowd had stopped, went in to see him at the same time as an adjutant who informed the count that the horses were harnessed. They were both pale, and the superintendent of police, after reporting that he had executed the instructions he had received, informed the count that an immense crowd had collected in the courtyard and wished to see him.

Without saying a word Rostopchín rose and walked hastily to his light, luxurious drawing room, went to the balcony door, took hold of the handle, let it go again, and went to the window from which he had a better view of the whole crowd. The tall lad was standing in front, flourishing his arm and saying something with a stern look. The blood-stained smith stood beside him with a gloomy face. A drone of voices was audible through the closed window.

"Is my carriage ready?" asked Rostopchín, stepping back from the window.

"It is, your excellency," replied the adjutant.

Rostopchín went again to the balcony door.

"But what do they want?" he asked the superintendent of police.

"Your excellency, they say they have got ready, according to your orders, to go against the French, and they shouted something about treachery. But it is a turbulent crowd, your excellency—I hardly managed to get away from it. Your excellency, I venture to suggest..."

"You may go. I don't need you to tell me what to do!" exclaimed Rostopchín angrily.

He stood by the balcony door looking at the crowd.

"This is what they have done with Russia! This is what they have done with me!" thought he, full of an irrepressible fury that welled up within him against the someone to whom what was happening might be attributed. As often happens with passionate people, he was mastered by anger but was still seeking an object on which to vent it. "Here is that mob, the dregs of the people," he thought as he gazed at the crowd: "this rabble they have roused by their folly! They want a victim," he thought as he looked at the tall lad flourishing his arm. And this thought occurred to him just because he himself desired a victim, something on which to vent his rage.

"Is the carriage ready?" he asked again.

"Yes, your excellency. What are your orders about Vereshchágin? He is waiting at the porch," said the adjutant.

"Ah!" exclaimed Rostopchín, as if struck by an unexpected recollection.

And rapidly opening the door he went resolutely out onto the balcony. The talking instantly ceased, hats and caps were doffed, and all eyes were raised to the count.

"Good morning, lads!" said the count briskly and loudly. "Thank you for coming. I'll come out to you in a moment, but we must first settle with the villain. We must punish the villain who has caused the ruin of Moscow. Wait for me!"

And the count stepped as briskly back into the room and slammed the door behind him.

A murmur of approbation and satisfaction ran through the crowd. "He'll settle with all the villains, you'll see! And you said the French... He'll show you what law is!" the mob were saying as if reproving one another for their lack of confidence.

A few minutes later an officer came hurriedly out of the front door, gave an order, and the dragoons formed up in line. The crowd moved eagerly from the balcony toward the porch. Rostopchín, coming out there with quick angry steps, looked hastily around as if seeking someone.

"Where is he?" he inquired. And as he spoke he saw a young man coming round the corner of the house between two dragoons. He had a long thin neck, and his head, that had been half shaved, was again covered by short hair. This young man was dressed in a threadbare blue cloth coat lined with fox fur, that had once been smart, and dirty hempen convict trousers, over which were pulled his thin, dirty, trodden-down boots. On his thin, weak legs were heavy chains which hampered his irresolute movements.

"Ah!" said Rostopchín, hurriedly turning away his eyes from the young man in the fur-lined coat and pointing to the bottom step of the porch. "Put him there."

The young man in his clattering chains stepped clumsily to the spot indicated, holding away with one finger the coat collar which chafed his neck, turned his long neck twice this way and that, sighed, and submissively folded before him his thin hands, unused to work.

For several seconds while the young man was taking his place on the step the silence continued. Only among the back rows of the people, who were all pressing toward the one spot, could sighs, groans, and the shuffling of feet be heard.

While waiting for the young man to take his place on the step Rostopchín stood frowning and rubbing his face with his hand.

"Lads!" said he, with a metallic ring in his voice. "This man, Vereshchágin, is the scoundrel by whose doing Moscow is perishing."

The young man in the fur-lined coat, stooping a little, stood in a submissive attitude, his fingers clasped before him. His emaciated young face, disfigured by the half-shaven head, hung down hopelessly. At the count's first words he raised it slowly and looked up at him as if wishing to say something or at least to meet his eye. But Rostopchín did not look at him. A vein in the young man's long thin neck swelled like a cord and went blue behind the ear, and suddenly his face flushed.

All eyes were fixed on him. He looked at the crowd, and rendered more hopeful by the expression he read on the faces there, he smiled sadly and timidly, and lowering his head shifted his feet on the step.

"He has betrayed his Tsar and his country, he has gone over to Bonaparte. He alone of all the Russians has disgraced the Russian name, he has caused Moscow to perish," said Rostopchín in a sharp, even voice, but suddenly he glanced down at Vereshchágin who continued to stand in the same submissive attitude. As if inflamed by the sight, he raised his arm and addressed the people, almost shouting:

"Deal with him as you think fit! I hand him over to you."

The crowd remained silent and only pressed closer and closer to one another. To keep one another back, to breathe in that stifling atmosphere, to be unable to stir, and to await something unknown, uncomprehended, and terrible, was becoming unbearable. Those standing in front, who had seen and heard what had taken place before them, all stood with wide-open eyes and mouths, straining with all their strength, and held back the crowd that was pushing behind them.

"Beat him!... Let the traitor perish and not disgrace the Russian name!" shouted Rostopchín. "Cut him down. I command it."

Hearing not so much the words as the angry tone of Rostopchín's voice, the crowd moaned and heaved forward, but again paused.

"Count!" exclaimed the timid yet theatrical voice of Vereshchágin in the midst of the momentary silence that ensued, "Count! One God is above us both...." He lifted his head and again the thick vein in his thin neck filled with blood and the color rapidly came and went in his face.

He did not finish what he wished to say.

"Cut him down! I command it..." shouted Rostopchín, suddenly growing pale like Vereshchágin.

"Draw sabers!" cried the dragoon officer, drawing his own.

Another still stronger wave flowed through the crowd and reaching the front ranks carried it swaying to the very steps of the porch. The tall youth, with a stony look on his face, and rigid and uplifted arm, stood beside Vereshchágin.

"Saber him!" the dragoon officer almost whispered.

And one of the soldiers, his face all at once distorted with fury, struck Vereshchágin on the head with the blunt side of his saber.

"Ah!" cried Vereshchágin in meek surprise, looking round with a frightened glance as if not understanding why this was done to him. A similar moan of surprise and horror ran through the crowd. "O Lord!" exclaimed a sorrowful voice.

But after the exclamation of surprise that had escaped from Vereshchágin he uttered a plaintive cry of pain, and that cry was fatal. The barrier of human feeling, strained to the utmost, that had held the crowd in check suddenly broke. The crime had begun and must now be completed. The plaintive moan of reproach was drowned by the threatening and angry roar of the crowd. Like the seventh and last wave that shatters a ship, that last irresistible wave burst from the rear and reached the front ranks, carrying them off their feet and engulfing them all. The dragoon was about to repeat his blow. Vereshchágin with a cry of horror, covering his head with his hands, rushed toward the crowd. The tall youth, against whom he stumbled, seized his thin neck with his hands and, yelling wildly, fell with him under the feet of the pressing, struggling crowd.

Some beat and tore at Vereshchágin, others at the tall youth. And the screams of those that were being trampled on and of those who tried to rescue the tall lad only increased the fury of the crowd. It was a long time before the dragoons could extricate the bleeding youth, beaten almost to death. And for a long time, despite the feverish haste with which the mob tried to end the work that had been begun, those who were hitting, throttling, and tearing at Vereshchágin were unable to kill him, for the crowd pressed from all sides, swaying as one mass with them in the center and rendering it impossible for them either to kill him or let him go.

"Hit him with an ax, eh!... Crushed?... Traitor, he sold Christ.... Still alive... tenacious... serves him right! Torture serves a thief right. Use the hatchet!... What—still alive?"

Only when the victim ceased to struggle and his cries changed to a long-drawn, measured death rattle did the crowd around his prostrate, bleeding corpse begin rapidly to change places. Each one came up, glanced at what had been done, and with horror, reproach, and astonishment pushed back again.

"O Lord! The people are like wild beasts! How could he be alive?" voices in the crowd could be heard saying. "Quite a young fellow too... must have been a merchant's son. What men!... and they say he's not the right one.... How not the right one?... O Lord! And there's another has been beaten too—they say he's nearly done for.... Oh, the people... Aren't they afraid of sinning?..." said the same mob now, looking with pained distress at the dead body with its long, thin, half-severed neck and its livid face stained with blood and dust.

A painstaking police officer, considering the presence of a corpse in his excellency's courtyard unseemly, told the dragoons to take it away. Two dragoons took it by its distorted legs and dragged it along the ground. The gory, dust-stained, half-shaven head with its long neck trailed twisting along the ground. The crowd shrank back from it.

At the moment when Vereshchágin fell and the crowd closed in with savage yells and swayed about him, Rostopchín suddenly turned pale and, instead of going to the back entrance where his carriage awaited him, went with hurried steps and bent head, not knowing where and why, along the passage leading to the rooms on the ground floor. The count's face was white and he could not control the feverish twitching of his lower jaw.

"This way, your excellency... Where are you going?... This way, please..." said a trembling, frightened voice behind him.

Count Rostopchín was unable to reply and, turning obediently, went in the direction indicated. At the back entrance stood his *calèche*. The distant roar of the yelling crowd was audible even there. He hastily took his seat and told the coachman to drive him to his country house in Sokólniki.

When they reached the Myasnítski Street and could no longer hear the shouts of the mob, the count began to repent. He remembered with dissatisfaction the agitation and fear he had betrayed before his subordinates. "The mob is terrible—disgusting," he said to himself in French. "They are like wolves whom nothing but flesh can appease." "Count! One God is above us both!"—Vereshchágin's words suddenly recurred to him, and a disagreeable shiver ran down his back. But this was only a momentary feeling and Count Rostopchín smiled disdainfully at himself. "I had other duties," thought he. "The people had to be appeased. Many other victims have perished and are perishing for the public good"—and he began thinking of his social duties to his family and to the city entrusted to him, and of himself—not himself as Theodore VasílyevichRostopchín (he fancied that Theodore VasílyevichRostopchín was sacrificing himself for the public good) but himself as governor, the representative of authority and of the Tsar. "Had I been simply Theodore Vasílyevich my course of action would have been quite different, but it was my duty to safeguard my life and dignity as commander in chief."

Lightly swaying on the flexible springs of his carriage and no longer hearing the terrible sounds of the crowd, Rostopchín grew physically calm and, as always happens, as soon as he became physically tranquil his mind devised reasons why he should be mentally tranquil too. The thought which tranquillized Rostopchín was not a new one. Since the world began and men have killed one another no one has ever committed such a crime against his fellow man without comforting himself with this same idea. This idea is *le bien public*, the hypothetical welfare of other people.

To a man not swayed by passion that welfare is never certain, but he who commits such a crime always knows just where that welfare lies. And Rostopchín now knew it.

Not only did his reason not reproach him for what he had done, but he even found cause for self-satisfaction in having so successfully contrived to avail himself of a convenient opportunity to punish a criminal and at the same time pacify the mob.

"Vereshchágin was tried and condemned to death," thought Rostopchín (though the Senate had only condemned Vereshchágin to hard labor), "he was a traitor and a spy. I could not let him go unpunished and so I have killed two birds with one stone: to appease the mob I gave them a victim and at the same time punished a miscreant."

Having reached his country house and begun to give orders about domestic arrangements, the count grew quite tranquil.

Half an hour later he was driving with his fast horses across the Sokólniki field, no longer thinking of what had occurred but considering what was to come. He was driving to the Yaúza bridge where he had heard that Kutúzov was. Count Rostopchín was mentally preparing the angry and stinging reproaches he meant to address to Kutúzov for his deception. He would make that foxy old courtier feel that the responsibility for all the calamities that would follow the abandonment of the city and the ruin of Russia (as Rostopchín regarded it) would fall upon his doting old head. Planning beforehand what he would say to Kutúzov, Rostopchín turned angrily in his *calèche* and gazed sternly from side to side.

The Sokólniki field was deserted. Only at the end of it, in front of the almshouse and the lunatic asylum, could be seen some people in white and others like them walking singly across the field shouting and gesticulating.

One of these was running to cross the path of Count Rostopchín's carriage, and the count himself, his coachman, and his dragoons looked with vague horror and curiosity at these released lunatics and especially at the one running toward them.

Swaying from side to side on his long, thin legs in his fluttering dressing gown, this lunatic was running impetuously, his gaze fixed on Rostopchín, shouting something in a hoarse voice and making signs to him to stop. The lunatic's solemn, gloomy face was thin and yellow, with its beard growing in uneven tufts. His black, agate pupils with saffron-yellow whites moved restlessly near the lower eyelids.

"Stop! Pull up, I tell you!" he cried in a piercing voice, and again shouted something breathlessly with emphatic intonations and gestures.

Coming abreast of the *calèche* he ran beside it.

"Thrice have they slain me, thrice have I risen from the dead. They stoned me, crucified me... I shall rise... shall rise... shall rise. They have torn my body. The kingdom of God will be overthrown... Thrice will I overthrow it and thrice re-establish it!" he cried, raising his voice higher and higher.

Count Rostopchín suddenly grew pale as he had done when the crowd closed in on Vereshchágin. He turned away. "Go fas... faster!" he cried in a trembling voice to his coachman. The *calèche* flew over the ground as fast as the horses could draw it, but for a long time Count Rostopchín still heard the insane despairing screams growing fainter in the distance, while his eyes saw nothing but the astonished, frightened, bloodstained face of "the traitor" in the fur-lined coat.

Recent as that mental picture was, Rostopchín already felt that it had cut deep into his heart and drawn blood. Even now he felt clearly that the gory trace of that recollection would not pass with time, but that the terrible memory would, on the contrary, dwell in his heart ever more cruelly and painfully to the end of his life. He seemed still to hear the sound of his own words: "Cut him down! I command it...."

"Why did I utter those words? It was by some accident I said them.... I need not have said them," he thought. "And then nothing would have happened." He saw the frightened and then infuriated face of the dragoon who dealt the blow, the look of silent, timid reproach that boy in the fur-lined coat had turned upon him. "But I did not do it for my own sake. I was bound to act that way.... The mob, the traitor... the public welfare," thought he.

Troops were still crowding at the Yaúza bridge. It was hot. Kutúzov, dejected and frowning, sat on a bench by the bridge toying with his whip in the sand when a *calèche* dashed up noisily. A man in a general's uniform with plumes in his hat went up to Kutúzov and said something in French. It was Count Rostopchín. He told Kutúzov that he had come because Moscow, the capital, was no more and only the army remained.

"Things would have been different if your Serene Highness had not told me that you would not abandon Moscow without another battle; all this would not have happened," he said.

Kutúzov looked at Rostopchín as if, not grasping what was said to him, he was trying to read something peculiar written at that moment on the face of the man addressing him. Rostopchín grew confused and became silent. Kutúzov slightly shook his head and not taking his penetrating gaze from Rostopchín's face muttered softly:

"No! I shall not give up Moscow without a battle!"

Whether Kutúzov was thinking of something entirely different when he spoke those words, or uttered them purposely, knowing them to be meaningless, at any rate Rostopchín made no reply and hastily left him. And strange to say, the Governor of Moscow, the proud Count Rostopchín, took up a Cossack whip and went to the bridge where he began with shouts to drive on the carts that blocked the way.

CHAPTER XXVI

Toward four o'clock in the afternoon Murat's troops were entering Moscow. In front rode a detachment of Württemberg hussars and behind them rode the King of Naples himself accompanied by a numerous suite.

About the middle of the Arbát Street, near the Church of the Miraculous Icon of St. Nicholas, Murat halted to await news from the advanced detachment as to the condition in which they had found the citadel, *le Kremlin*.

Around Murat gathered a group of those who had remained in Moscow. They all stared in timid bewilderment at the strange, long-haired commander dressed up in feathers and gold.

"Is that their Tsar himself? He's not bad!" low voices could be heard saying.

An interpreter rode up to the group.

"Take off your cap... your caps!" These words went from one to another in the crowd. The interpreter addressed an old porter and asked if it was far to the Krémlin. The porter, listening in perplexity to the unfamiliar Polish accent and not realizing that the interpreter was speaking Russian, did not understand what was being said to him and slipped behind the others.

Murat approached the interpreter and told him to ask where the Russian army was. One of the Russians understood what was asked and several voices at once began answering the interpreter. A French officer, returning from the advanced detachment, rode up to Murat and reported that the gates of the citadel had been barricaded and that there was probably an ambuscade there.

"Good!" said Murat and, turning to one of the gentlemen in his suite, ordered four light guns to be moved forward to fire at the gates.

The guns emerged at a trot from the column following Murat and advanced up the Arbát. When they reached the end of the Vozdvízhenka Street they halted and drew in the Square. Several French officers superintended the placing of the guns and looked at the Krémlin through field glasses.

The bells in the Krémlin were ringing for vespers, and this sound troubled the French. They imagined it to be a call to arms. A few infantrymen ran to the Kutáfyev Gate. Beams and wooden screens had been put there, and two musket shots rang out from under the gate as soon as an officer and men began to run toward it. A general who was standing by the guns shouted some words of command to the officer, and the latter ran back again with his men.

The sound of three more shots came from the gate.

One shot struck a French soldier's foot, and from behind the screens came the strange sound of a few voices shouting. Instantly as at a word of command the expression of cheerful serenity on the faces of the French general, officers, and men changed to one of determined concentrated readiness for strife and suffering. To all of them from the marshal to the least soldier, that place was not the Vozdvízhenka, Mokhaváya, or Kutáfyev Street, nor the Tróitsa Gate (places familiar in Moscow), but a new battlefield which would probably prove sanguinary. And all made ready for that battle. The cries from the gates ceased. The guns were advanced, the artillerymen blew the ash off their linstocks, and an officer gave the word "Fire!" This was followed by two whistling sounds of canister shot, one after another. The shot rattled against the stone of the gate and upon the wooden beams and screens, and two wavering clouds of smoke rose over the Square.

A few instants after the echo of the reports resounding over the stone-built Krémlin had died away the French heard a strange sound above their head. Thousands of crows rose above the walls and circled in the air, cawing and noisily flapping their wings. Together with that sound came a solitary human cry from the gateway and amid the smoke appeared the figure of a bareheaded man in a peasant's coat.

He grasped a musket and took aim at the French. "Fire!" repeated the officer once more, and the reports of a musket and of two cannon shots were heard simultaneously. The gate was again hidden by smoke.

Nothing more stirred behind the screens and the French infantry soldiers and officers advanced to the gate. In the gateway lay three wounded and four dead. Two men in peasant coats ran away at the foot of the wall, toward the Známenka.

"Clear that away!" said the officer, pointing to the beams and the corpses, and the French soldiers, after dispatching the wounded, threw the corpses over the parapet.

Who these men were nobody knew. "Clear that away!" was all that was said of them, and they were thrown over the parapet and removed later on that they might not stink. Thiers alone dedicates a few eloquent lines to their memory: "These wretches had occupied the sacred citadel, having supplied themselves with guns from the arsenal, and fired" (the wretches) "at the French. Some of them were sabered and the Krémlin was purged of their presence."

Murat was informed that the way had been cleared. The French entered the gates and began pitching their camp in the Senate Square. Out of the windows of the Senate House the soldiers threw chairs into the Square for fuel and kindled fires there.

Other detachments passed through the Krémlin and encamped along the Moroséyka, the Lubyánka, and Pokróvka Streets. Others quartered themselves along the Vozdvízhenka, the Nikólski, and the Tverskóy Streets. No masters of the houses being found anywhere, the French were not billeted on the inhabitants as is usual in towns but lived in it as in a camp.

Though tattered, hungry, worn out, and reduced to a third of their original number, the French entered Moscow in good marching order. It was a weary and famished, but still a fighting and menacing army. But it remained an army only until its soldiers had dispersed into their different lodgings. As soon as the men of the various regiments began to disperse among the wealthy and deserted houses, the army was lost forever and there came into being something nondescript, neither citizens nor soldiers but what are known as marauders. When five weeks later these same men left Moscow, they no longer formed an army. They were a mob of marauders, each carrying a quantity of articles which seemed to him valuable or useful. The aim of each man when he left Moscow was no longer, as it had been, to conquer, but merely to keep what he had acquired. Like a monkey which puts its paw into the narrow neck of a jug, and having seized a handful of nuts will not open its fist for fear of losing what it holds, and therefore perishes, the French when they left Moscow had inevitably to perish because they carried their loot with them, yet to abandon what they had stolen was as impossible for them as it is for the monkey to open its paw and let go of its nuts. Ten minutes after each regiment had entered a Moscow district, not a soldier or officer was left. Men in military uniforms and Hessian boots could be seen through the windows, laughing and walking through the rooms. In cellars and storerooms similar men were busy among the provisions, and in the yards unlocking or breaking open coach house and stable doors, lighting fires in kitchens and kneading and baking bread with rolled-up sleeves, and cooking; or frightening, amusing, or caressing women and children. There were many such men both in the shops and houses—but there was no army.

Order after order was issued by the French commanders that day forbidding the men to disperse about the town, sternly forbidding any violence to the inhabitants or any looting, and announcing a roll call for that very evening. But despite all these measures the men, who had till then constituted an army, flowed all over the wealthy, deserted city with its comforts and plentiful supplies. As a hungry herd of cattle keeps well together when crossing a barren field, but gets out of hand and at once disperses uncontrollably as soon as it reaches rich pastures, so did the army disperse all over the wealthy city.

No residents were left in Moscow, and the soldiers—like water percolating through sand—spread irresistibly through the city in all directions from the Krémlin into which they had first marched. The cavalry, on entering a merchant's house that had been abandoned and finding there stabling more than sufficient for their horses, went on, all the same, to the next house which seemed to them better. Many of them appropriated several houses, chalked their names on them, and quarreled and even fought with other companies for them. Before they had had time to secure quarters the soldiers ran out into the streets to see the city and, hearing that everything had been abandoned, rushed to places where valuables were to be had for the taking. The officers followed to check the soldiers and were involuntarily drawn into doing the same. In Carriage Row carriages had been left in the shops, and generals flocked there to select *calèches* and coaches for themselves. The few inhabitants who had remained invited commanding officers to their houses, hoping thereby to secure themselves from being plundered. There were masses of wealth and there seemed no end to it. All around the quarters occupied by the French were other regions still unexplored and unoccupied where, they thought, yet greater riches might be found. And Moscow engulfed the army ever deeper and deeper. When water is spilled on dry ground both the dry ground and the water disappear and mud results; and in the same way the entry of the famished army into the rich and deserted city resulted in fires and looting and the destruction of both the army and the wealthy city.

The French attributed the Fire of Moscow *au patriotismeféroce de Rostopchíne*, * the Russians to the barbarity of the French. In reality, however, it was not, and could not be, possible to explain the burning of Moscow by making any individual, or any group of people, responsible for it. Moscow was burned because it found itself in a position in which any town built of wood was bound to burn, quite apart from whether it had, or had not, a hundred and thirty inferior fire engines. Deserted Moscow had to burn as inevitably as a heap of shavings has to burn on which sparks continually fall for several days. A town built of wood, where scarcely a day passes without conflagrations when the house owners are in residence and a police force is present, cannot help burning when its inhabitants have left it and it is occupied by soldiers who smoke pipes, make campfires of the Senate chairs in the Senate Square, and cook themselves meals twice a day. In peacetime it is only necessary to billet troops in the villages of any district and the number of fires in that district immediately increases. How much then must the probability of fire be increased in an abandoned, wooden town where foreign troops are quartered. "*Le patriotismeféroce de Rostopchíne*" and the barbarity of the French were not to blame in the matter. Moscow was set on fire by the soldiers' pipes, kitchens, and campfires, and by the carelessness of enemy soldiers occupying houses they did not own. Even if there was any arson (which is very doubtful, for no one had any reason to burn the houses—in any case a troublesome and dangerous thing to do),

---

arson cannot be regarded as the cause, for the same thing would have happened without any incendiarism.

* To Rostopchín's ferocious patriotism.

However tempting it might be for the French to blame Rostopchín's ferocity and for Russians to blame the scoundrel Bonaparte, or later on to place an heroic torch in the hands of their own people, it is impossible not to see that there could be no such direct cause of the fire, for Moscow had to burn as every village, factory, or house must burn which is left by its owners and in which strangers are allowed to live and cook their porridge. Moscow was burned by its inhabitants, it is true, but by those who had abandoned it and not by those who remained in it. Moscow when occupied by the enemy did not remain intact like Berlin, Vienna, and other towns, simply because its inhabitants abandoned it and did not welcome the French with bread and salt, nor bring them the keys of the city.

CHAPTER XXVII

The absorption of the French by Moscow, radiating starwise as it did, only reached the quarter where Pierre was staying by the evening of the second of September.

After the last two days spent in solitude and unusual circumstances, Pierre was in a state bordering on insanity. He was completely obsessed by one persistent thought. He did not know how or when this thought had taken such possession of him, but he remembered nothing of the past, understood nothing of the present, and all he saw and heard appeared to him like a dream.

He had left home only to escape the intricate tangle of life's demands that enmeshed him, and which in his present condition he was unable to unravel. He had gone to Joseph Alexéevich's house, on the plea of sorting the deceased's books and papers, only in search of rest from life's turmoil, for in his mind the memory of Joseph Alexéevich was connected with a world of eternal, solemn, and calm thoughts, quite contrary to the restless confusion into which he felt himself being drawn. He sought a quiet refuge, and in Joseph Alexéevich's study he really found it. When he sat with his elbows on the dusty writing table in the deathlike stillness of the study, calm and significant memories of the last few days rose one after another in his imagination, particularly of the battle of Borodinó and of that vague sense of his own insignificance and insincerity compared with the truth, simplicity, and strength of the class of men he mentally classed as *they*. When Gerásim roused him from his reverie the idea occurred to him of taking part in the popular defense of Moscow which he knew was projected. And with that object he had asked Gerásim to get him a peasant's coat and a pistol, confiding to him his intentions of remaining in Joseph Aléxeevich's house and keeping his name secret. Then during the first day spent in inaction and solitude (he tried several times to fix his attention on the Masonic manuscripts, but was unable to do so) the idea that had previously occurred to him of the cabalistic significance of his name in connection with Bonaparte's more than once vaguely presented itself. But the idea that he, *L'russeBesuhof*, was destined to set a limit to the power of the *Beast* was as yet only one of the fancies that often passed through his mind and left no trace behind.

When, having bought the coat merely with the object of taking part among the people in the defense of Moscow, Pierre had met the Rostóvs and Natásha had said to him: "Are you remaining in Moscow?... How splendid!" the thought flashed into his mind that it really would be a good thing, even if Moscow were taken, for him to remain there and do what he was predestined to do.

Next day, with the sole idea of not sparing himself and not lagging in any way behind *them*, Pierre went to the Three Hills gate. But when he returned to the house convinced that Moscow would not be defended, he suddenly felt that what before had seemed to him merely a possibility had now become absolutely necessary and inevitable. He must remain in Moscow, concealing his name, and must meet Napoleon and kill him, and either perish or put an end to the misery of all Europe—which it seemed to him was solely due to Napoleon.

Pierre knew all the details of the attempt on Bonaparte's life in 1809 by a German student in Vienna, and knew that the student had been shot. And the risk to which he would expose his life by carrying out his design excited him still more.

Two equally strong feelings drew Pierre irresistibly to this purpose. The first was a feeling of the necessity of sacrifice and suffering in view of the common calamity, the same feeling that had caused him to go to Mozháysk on the twenty-fifth and to make his way to the very thick of the battle and had now caused him to run away from his home and, in place of the luxury and comfort to which he was accustomed, to sleep on a hard sofa without undressing and eat the same food as Gerásim. The other was that vague and quite Russian feeling of contempt for everything conventional, artificial, and human—for everything the majority of men regard as the greatest good in the world. Pierre had first experienced this strange and fascinating feeling at the Slobóda Palace, when he had suddenly felt that wealth, power, and life—all that men so painstakingly acquire and guard—if it has any worth has so only by reason of the joy with which it can all be renounced.

It was the feeling that induces a volunteer recruit to spend his last penny on drink, and a drunken man to smash mirrors or glasses for no apparent reason and knowing that it will cost him all the money he possesses: the feeling which causes a man to perform actions which from an ordinary point of view are insane, to test, as it were, his personal power and strength, affirming the existence of a higher, nonhuman criterion of life.

From the very day Pierre had experienced this feeling for the first time at the Slobóda Palace he had been continuously under its influence, but only now found full satisfaction for it. Moreover, at this moment Pierre was supported in his design and prevented from renouncing it by what he had already done in that direction. If he were now to leave Moscow like everyone else, his flight from home, the peasant coat, the pistol, and his announcement to the Rostóvs that he would remain in Moscow would all become not merely meaningless but contemptible and ridiculous, and to this Pierre was very sensitive.

Pierre's physical condition, as is always the case, corresponded to his mental state. The unaccustomed coarse food, the vodka he drank during those days, the absence of wine and cigars, his dirty unchanged linen, two almost sleepless nights passed on a short sofa without bedding—all this kept him in a state of excitement bordering on insanity.

It was two o'clock in the afternoon. The French had already entered Moscow. Pierre knew this, but instead of acting he only thought about his undertaking, going over its minutest details in his mind. In his fancy he did not clearly picture to himself either the striking of the blow or the death of Napoleon, but with extraordinary vividness and melancholy enjoyment imagined his own destruction and heroic endurance.

"Yes, alone, for the sake of all, I must do it or perish!" he thought. "Yes, I will approach... and then suddenly... with pistol or dagger? But that is all the same! 'It is not I but the hand of Providence that punishes thee,' I shall say," thought he, imagining what he would say when killing Napoleon. "Well then, take me and execute me!" he went on, speaking to himself and bowing his head with a sad but firm expression.

While Pierre, standing in the middle of the room, was talking to himself in this way, the study door opened and on the threshold appeared the figure of MakárAlexéevich, always so timid before but now quite transformed.

His dressing gown was unfastened, his face red and distorted. He was obviously drunk. On seeing Pierre he grew confused at first, but noticing embarrassment on Pierre's face immediately grew bold and, staggering on his thin legs, advanced into the middle of the room.

"They're frightened," he said confidentially in a hoarse voice. "I say I won't surrender, I say... Am I not right, sir?"

He paused and then suddenly seeing the pistol on the table seized it with unexpected rapidity and ran out into the corridor.

Gerásim and the porter, who had followed MakárAlexéevich, stopped him in the vestibule and tried to take the pistol from him. Pierre, coming out into the corridor, looked with pity and repulsion at the half-crazy old man. MakárAlexéevich, frowning with exertion, held on to the pistol and screamed hoarsely, evidently with some heroic fancy in his head.

"To arms! Board them! No, you shan't get it," he yelled.

"That will do, please, that will do. Have the goodness—please, sir, to let go! Please, sir..." pleaded Gerásim, trying carefully to steer MakárAlexéevich by the elbows back to the door.

"Who are you? Bonaparte!..." shouted MakárAlexéevich.

"That's not right, sir. Come to your room, please, and rest. Allow me to have the pistol."

"Be off, thou base slave! Touch me not! See this?" shouted MakárAlexéevich, brandishing the pistol. "Board them!"

"Catch hold!" whispered Gerásim to the porter.

They seized MakárAlexéevich by the arms and dragged him to the door.

The vestibule was filled with the discordant sounds of a struggle and of a tipsy, hoarse voice.

Suddenly a fresh sound, a piercing feminine scream, reverberated from the porch and the cook came running into the vestibule.

"It's them! Gracious heavens! O Lord, four of them, horsemen!" she cried.

Gerásim and the porter let MakárAlexéevich go, and in the now silent corridor the sound of several hands knocking at the front door could be heard.

CHAPTER XXVIII

P ierre, having decided that until he had carried out his design he would disclose neither his identity nor his knowledge of French, stood at the half-open door of the corridor, intending to conceal himself as soon as the French entered. But the French entered and still Pierre did not retire—an irresistible curiosity kept him there.

There were two of them. One was an officer—a tall, soldierly, handsome man—the other evidently a private or an orderly, sunburned, short, and thin, with sunken cheeks and a dull expression. The officer walked in front, leaning on a stick and slightly limping. When he had advanced a few steps he stopped, having apparently decided that these were good quarters, turned round to the soldiers standing at the entrance, and in a loud voice of command ordered them to put up the horses. Having done that, the officer, lifting his elbow with a smart gesture, stroked his mustache and lightly touched his hat.

"*Bonjour, la compagnie!*" * said he gaily, smiling and looking about him.

* "Good day, everybody!"

No one gave any reply.

"*Vousêtes le bourgeois?*" * the officer asked Gerásim.

* "Are you the master here?"

Gerásim gazed at the officer with an alarmed and inquiring look.

"*Quartier, quartier, logement!*" said the officer, looking down at the little man with a condescending and good-natured smile. "*Les* *françaissont de bons enfants. Que diable! Voyons! Ne nous fâchons pas, monvieux!"* * added he, clapping the scared and silent Gerásim on the shoulder. "Well, does no one speak French in this establishment?" he asked again in French, looking around and meeting Pierre's eyes. Pierre moved away from the door.

* "Quarters, quarters, lodgings! The French are good fellows. What the devil! There, don't let us be cross, old fellow!"

Again the officer turned to Gerásim and asked him to show him the rooms in the house.

"Master, not here—don't understand... me, you..." said Gerásim, trying to render his words more comprehensible by contorting them.

Still smiling, the French officer spread out his hands before Gerásim's nose, intimating that he did not understand him either, and moved, limping, to the door at which Pierre was standing. Pierre wished to go away and conceal himself, but at that moment he saw MakárAlexéevich appearing at the open kitchen door with the pistol in his hand. With a madman's cunning, MakárAlexéevich eyed the Frenchman, raised his pistol, and took aim.

"Board them!" yelled the tipsy man, trying to press the trigger. Hearing the yell the officer turned round, and at the same moment Pierre threw himself on the drunkard. Just when Pierre snatched at and struck up the pistol MakárAlexéevich at last got his fingers on the trigger, there was a deafening report, and all were enveloped in a cloud of smoke. The Frenchman turned pale and rushed to the door.

Forgetting his intention of concealing his knowledge of French, Pierre, snatching away the pistol and throwing it down, ran up to the officer and addressed him in French.

"You are not wounded?" he asked.

"I think not," answered the Frenchman, feeling himself over. "But I have had a lucky escape this time," he added, pointing to the damaged plaster of the wall. "Who is that man?" said he, looking sternly at Pierre.

"Oh, I am really in despair at what has occurred," said Pierre rapidly, quite forgetting the part he had intended to play. "He is an unfortunate madman who did not know what he was doing."

The officer went up to MakárAlexéevich and took him by the collar.

MakárAlexéevich was standing with parted lips, swaying, as if about to fall asleep, as he leaned against the wall.

"Brigand! You shall pay for this," said the Frenchman, letting go of him. "We French are merciful after victory, but we do not pardon traitors," he added, with a look of gloomy dignity and a fine energetic gesture.

Pierre continued, in French, to persuade the officer not to hold that drunken imbecile to account. The Frenchman listened in silence with the same gloomy expression, but suddenly turned to Pierre with a smile. For a few seconds he looked at him in silence. His handsome face assumed a melodramatically gentle expression and he held out his hand.

"You have saved my life. You are French," said he.

For a Frenchman that deduction was indubitable. Only a Frenchman could perform a great deed, and to save his life—the life of M. Ramballe, captain of the 13th Light Regiment—was undoubtedly a very great deed.

But however indubitable that conclusion and the officer's conviction based upon it, Pierre felt it necessary to disillusion him.

"I am Russian," he said quickly.

"Tut, tut, tut! Tell that to others," said the officer, waving his finger before his nose and smiling. "You shall tell me all about that presently. I am delighted to meet a compatriot. Well, and what are we to do with this man?" he added, addressing himself to Pierre as to a brother.

Even if Pierre were not a Frenchman, having once received that loftiest of human appellations he could not renounce it, said the officer's look and tone. In reply to his last question Pierre again explained who MakárAlexéevich was and how just before their arrival that drunken imbecile had seized the loaded pistol which they had not had time to recover from him, and begged the officer to let the deed go unpunished.

The Frenchman expanded his chest and made a majestic gesture with his arm.

"You have saved my life! You are French. You ask his pardon? I grant it you. Lead that man away!" said he quickly and energetically, and taking the arm of Pierre whom he had promoted to be a Frenchman for saving his life, he went with him into the room.

The soldiers in the yard, hearing the shot, came into the passage asking what had happened, and expressed their readiness to punish the culprits, but the officer sternly checked them.

"You will be called in when you are wanted," he said.

The soldiers went out again, and the orderly, who had meanwhile had time to visit the kitchen, came up to his officer.

"Captain, there is soup and a leg of mutton in the kitchen," said he. "Shall I serve them up?"

"Yes, and some wine," answered the captain.

CHAPTER XXIX

When the French officer went into the room with Pierre the latter again thought it his duty to assure him that he was not French and wished to go away, but the officer would not hear of it. He was so very polite, amiable, good-natured, and genuinely grateful to Pierre for saving his life that Pierre had not the heart to refuse, and sat down with him in the parlor—the first room they entered. To Pierre's assurances that he was not a Frenchman, the captain, evidently not understanding how anyone could decline so flattering an appellation, shrugged his shoulders and said that if Pierre absolutely insisted on passing for a Russian let it be so, but for all that he would be forever bound to Pierre by gratitude for saving his life.

Had this man been endowed with the slightest capacity for perceiving the feelings of others, and had he at all understood what Pierre's feelings were, the latter would probably have left him, but the man's animated obtuseness to everything other than himself disarmed Pierre.

"A Frenchman or a Russian prince incognito," said the officer, looking at Pierre's fine though dirty linen and at the ring on his finger. "I owe my life to you and offer you my friendship. A Frenchman never forgets either an insult or a service. I offer you my friendship. That is all I can say."

There was so much good nature and nobility (in the French sense of the word) in the officer's voice, in the expression of his face and in his gestures, that Pierre, unconsciously smiling in response to the Frenchman's smile, pressed the hand held out to him.

"Captain Ramballe, of the 13th Light Regiment, Chevalier of the Legion of Honor for the affair on the seventh of September," he introduced himself, a self-satisfied irrepressible smile puckering his lips under his mustache. "Will you now be so good as to tell me with whom I have the honor of conversing so pleasantly, instead of being in the ambulance with that maniac's bullet in my body?"

Pierre replied that he could not tell him his name and, blushing, began to try to invent a name and to say something about his reason for concealing it, but the Frenchman hastily interrupted him.

"Oh, please!" said he. "I understand your reasons. You are an officer... a superior officer perhaps. You have borne arms against us. That's not my business. I owe you my life. That is enough for me. I am quite at your service. You belong to the gentry?" he concluded with a shade of inquiry in his tone. Pierre bent his head. "Your baptismal name, if you please. That is all I ask. Monsieur Pierre, you say.... That's all I want to know."

When the mutton and an omelet had been served and a samovar and vodka brought, with some wine which the French had taken from a Russian cellar and brought with them, Ramballe invited Pierre to share his dinner, and himself began to eat greedily and quickly like a healthy and hungry man, munching his food rapidly with his strong teeth, continually smacking his lips, and repeating—"Excellent! Delicious!" His face grew red and was covered with perspiration. Pierre was hungry and shared the dinner with pleasure. Morel, the orderly, brought some hot water in a saucepan and placed a bottle of claret in it. He also brought a bottle of kvass, taken from the kitchen for them to try. That beverage was already known to the French and had been given a special name. They called it *limonade de cochon* (pig's lemonade), and Morel spoke well of the *limonade de cochon* he had found in the kitchen. But as the captain had the wine they had taken while passing through Moscow, he left the kvass to Morel and applied himself to the bottle of Bordeaux. He wrapped the bottle up to its neck in a table napkin and poured out wine for himself and for Pierre. The satisfaction of his hunger and the wine rendered the captain still more lively and he chatted incessantly all through dinner.

"Yes, my dear Monsieur Pierre, I owe you a fine votive candle for saving me from that maniac.... You see, I have bullets enough in my body already. Here is one I got at Wagram" (he touched his side) "and a second at Smolénsk"—he showed a scar on his cheek—"and this leg which as you see does not want to march, I got that on the seventh at the great battle of la Moskowa. *Sacré Dieu!* It was splendid! That deluge of fire was worth seeing. It was a tough job you set us there, my word! You may be proud of it! And on my honor, in spite of the cough I caught there, I should be ready to begin again. I pity those who did not see it."

"I was there," said Pierre.

"Bah, really? So much the better! You are certainly brave foes. The great redoubt held out well, by my pipe!" continued the Frenchman. "And you made us pay dear for it. I was at it three times—sure as I sit here. Three times we reached the guns and three times we were thrown back like cardboard figures. Oh, it was beautiful, Monsieur Pierre! Your grenadiers were splendid, by heaven! I saw them close up their ranks six times in succession and march as if on parade. Fine fellows! Our King of Naples, who knows what's what, cried 'Bravo!' Ha, ha! So you are one of us soldiers!" he added, smiling, after a momentary pause. "So much the better, so much the better, Monsieur Pierre! Terrible in battle... gallant... with the fair" (he winked and smiled), "that's what the French are, Monsieur Pierre, aren't they?"

The captain was so naïvely and good-humoredly gay, so real, and so pleased with himself that Pierre almost winked back as he looked merrily at him. Probably the word "gallant" turned the captain's thoughts to the state of Moscow.

"Apropos, tell me please, is it true that the women have all left Moscow? What a queer idea! What had they to be afraid of?"

"Would not the French ladies leave Paris if the Russians entered it?" asked Pierre.

"Ha, ha, ha!" The Frenchman emitted a merry, sanguine chuckle, patting Pierre on the shoulder. "What a thing to say!" he exclaimed. "Paris?... But Paris, Paris..."

"Paris—the capital of the world," Pierre finished his remark for him.

The captain looked at Pierre. He had a habit of stopping short in the middle of his talk and gazing intently with his laughing, kindly eyes.

"Well, if you hadn't told me you were Russian, I should have wagered that you were Parisian! You have that... I don't know what, that..." and having uttered this compliment, he again gazed at him in silence.

"I have been in Paris. I spent years there," said Pierre.

"Oh yes, one sees that plainly. Paris!... A man who doesn't know Paris is a savage. You can tell a Parisian two leagues off. Paris is Talma, la Duchénois, Potier, the Sorbonne, the boulevards," and noticing that his conclusion was weaker than what had gone before, he added quickly: "There is only one Paris in the world. You have been to Paris and have remained Russian. Well, I don't esteem you the less for it."

Under the influence of the wine he had drunk, and after the days he had spent alone with his depressing thoughts, Pierre involuntarily enjoyed talking with this cheerful and good-natured man.

"To return to your ladies—I hear they are lovely. What a wretched idea to go and bury themselves in the steppes when the French army is in Moscow. What a chance those girls have missed! Your peasants, now—that's another thing; but you civilized people, you ought to know us better than that. We took Vienna, Berlin, Madrid, Naples, Rome, Warsaw, all the world's capitals.... We are feared, but we are loved. We are nice to know. And then the Emperor..." he began, but Pierre interrupted him.

"The Emperor," Pierre repeated, and his face suddenly became sad and embarrassed, "is the Emperor...?"

"The Emperor? He is generosity, mercy, justice, order, genius— that's what the Emperor is! It is I, Ramballe, who tell you so.... I assure you I was his enemy eight years ago. My father was an emigrant count.... But that man has vanquished me. He has taken hold of me. I could not resist the sight of the grandeur and glory with which he has covered France. When I understood what he wanted—when I saw that he was preparing a bed of laurels for us, you know, I said to myself: 'That is a monarch,' and I devoted myself to him! So there! Oh yes, *moncher*, he is the greatest man of the ages past or future."

"Is he in Moscow?" Pierre stammered with a guilty look.

The Frenchman looked at his guilty face and smiled.

"No, he will make his entry tomorrow," he replied, and continued his talk.

Their conversation was interrupted by the cries of several voices at the gate and by Morel, who came to say that some Württemberg hussars had come and wanted to put up their horses in the yard where the captain's horses were. This difficulty had arisen chiefly because the hussars did not understand what was said to them in French.

The captain had their senior sergeant called in, and in a stern voice asked him to what regiment he belonged, who was his commanding officer, and by what right he allowed himself to claim quarters that were already occupied. The German who knew little French, answered the two first questions by giving the names of his regiment and of his commanding officer, but in reply to the third question which he did not understand said, introducing broken French into his own German, that he was the quartermaster of the regiment and his commander had ordered him to occupy all the houses one after another. Pierre, who knew German, translated what the German said to the captain and gave the captain's reply to the Württemberg hussar in German. When he had understood what was said to him, the German submitted and took his men elsewhere. The captain went out into the porch and gave some orders in a loud voice.

When he returned to the room Pierre was sitting in the same place as before, with his head in his hands. His face expressed suffering. He really was suffering at that moment. When the captain went out and he was left alone, suddenly he came to himself and realized the position he was in. It was not that Moscow had been taken or that the happy conquerors were masters in it and were patronizing him. Painful as that was it was not that which tormented Pierre at the moment. He was tormented by the consciousness of his own weakness. The few glasses of wine he had drunk and the conversation with this good-natured man had destroyed the mood of concentrated gloom in which he had spent the last few days and which was essential for the execution of his design. The pistol, dagger, and peasant coat were ready. Napoleon was to enter the town next day. Pierre still considered that it would be a useful and worthy action to slay the evildoer, but now he felt that he would not do it. He did not know why, but he felt a foreboding that he would not carry out his intention. He struggled against the confession of his weakness but dimly felt that he could not overcome it and that his former gloomy frame of mind, concerning vengeance, killing, and self-sacrifice, had been dispersed like dust by contact with the first man he met.

The captain returned to the room, limping slightly and whistling a tune.

The Frenchman's chatter which had previously amused Pierre now repelled him. The tune he was whistling, his gait, and the gesture with which he twirled his mustache, all now seemed offensive. "I will go away immediately. I won't say another word to him," thought Pierre. He thought this, but still sat in the same place. A strange feeling of weakness tied him to the spot; he wished to get up and go away, but could not do so.

The captain, on the other hand, seemed very cheerful. He paced up and down the room twice. His eyes shone and his mustache twitched as if he were smiling to himself at some amusing thought.

"The colonel of those Württembergers is delightful," he suddenly said. "He's a German, but a nice fellow all the same.... But he's a German." He sat down facing Pierre. "By the way, you know German, then?"

Pierre looked at him in silence.

"What is the German for 'shelter'?"

"Shelter?" Pierre repeated. "The German for shelter is *Unterkunft.*"

"How do you say it?" the captain asked quickly and doubtfully.

"Unterkunft," Pierre repeated.

"Onterkoff," said the captain and looked at Pierre for some seconds with laughing eyes. "These Germans are first-rate fools, don't you think so, Monsieur Pierre?" he concluded.

"Well, let's have another bottle of this Moscow Bordeaux, shall we? Morel will warm us up another little bottle. Morel!" he called out gaily.

Morel brought candles and a bottle of wine. The captain looked at Pierre by the candlelight and was evidently struck by the troubled expression on his companion's face. Ramballe, with genuine distress and sympathy in his face, went up to Pierre and bent over him.

"There now, we're sad," said he, touching Pierre's hand. "Have I upset you? No, really, have you anything against me?" he asked Pierre. "Perhaps it's the state of affairs?"

Pierre did not answer, but looked cordially into the Frenchman's eyes whose expression of sympathy was pleasing to him.

"Honestly, without speaking of what I owe you, I feel friendship for you. Can I do anything for you? Dispose of me. It is for life and death. I say it with my hand on my heart!" said he, striking his chest.

"Thank you," said Pierre.

The captain gazed intently at him as he had done when he learned that "shelter" was *Unterkunft* in German, and his face suddenly brightened.

"Well, in that case, I drink to our friendship!" he cried gaily, filling two glasses with wine.

Pierre took one of the glasses and emptied it. Ramballe emptied his too, again pressed Pierre's hand, and leaned his elbows on the table in a pensive attitude.

"Yes, my dear friend," he began, "such is fortune's caprice. Who would have said that I should be a soldier and a captain of dragoons in the service of Bonaparte, as we used to call him? Yet here I am in Moscow with him. I must tell you, *moncher*," he continued in the sad and measured tones of a man who intends to tell a long story, "that our name is one of the most ancient in France."

And with a Frenchman's easy and naïve frankness the captain told Pierre the story of his ancestors, his childhood, youth, and manhood, and all about his relations and his financial and family affairs, *"ma pauvremère"* playing of course an important part in the story.

"But all that is only life's setting, the real thing is love—love! Am I not right, Monsieur Pierre?" said he, growing animated. "Another glass?"

Pierre again emptied his glass and poured himself out a third.

"Oh, women, women!" and the captain, looking with glistening eyes at Pierre, began talking of love and of his love affairs.

There were very many of these, as one could easily believe, looking at the officer's handsome, self-satisfied face, and noting the eager enthusiasm with which he spoke of women. Though all Ramballe's love stories had the sensual character which Frenchmen regard as the special charm and poetry of love, yet he told his story with such sincere conviction that he alone had experienced and known all the charm of love and he described women so alluringly that Pierre listened to him with curiosity.

It was plain that *l'amour* which the Frenchman was so fond of was not that low and simple kind that Pierre had once felt for his wife, nor was it the romantic love stimulated by himself that he experienced for Natásha. (Ramballe despised both these kinds of love equally: the one he considered the "love of clodhoppers" and the other the "love of simpletons.") *L'amour* which the Frenchman worshiped consisted principally in the unnaturalness of his relation to the woman and in a combination of incongruities giving the chief charm to the feeling.

Thus the captain touchingly recounted the story of his love for a fascinating marquise of thirty-five and at the same time for a charming, innocent child of seventeen, daughter of the bewitching marquise. The conflict of magnanimity between the mother and the daughter, ending in the mother's sacrificing herself and offering her daughter in marriage to her lover, even now agitated the captain, though it was the memory of a distant past. Then he recounted an episode in which the husband played the part of the lover, and he—the lover—assumed the role of the husband, as well as several droll incidents from his recollections of Germany, where "shelter" is called *Unterkunft* and where the husbands eat sauerkraut and the young girls are "too blonde."

Finally, the latest episode in Poland still fresh in the captain's memory, and which he narrated with rapid gestures and glowing face, was of how he had saved the life of a Pole (in general, the saving of life continually occurred in the captain's stories) and the Pole had entrusted to him his enchanting wife (*parisienne de cœur*) while himself entering the French service. The captain was happy, the enchanting Polish lady wished to elope with him, but, prompted by magnanimity, the captain restored the wife to the husband, saying as he did so: "I have saved your life, and I save your honor!" Having repeated these words the captain wiped his eyes and gave himself a shake, as if driving away the weakness which assailed him at this touching recollection.

Listening to the captain's tales, Pierre—as often happens late in the evening and under the influence of wine—followed all that was told him, understood it all, and at the same time followed a train of personal memories which, he knew not why, suddenly arose in his mind. While listening to these love stories his own love for Natásha unexpectedly rose to his mind, and going over the pictures of that love in his imagination he mentally compared them with Ramballe's tales. Listening to the story of the struggle between love and duty, Pierre saw before his eyes every minutest detail of his last meeting with the object of his love at the Súkharev water tower. At the time of that meeting it had not produced an effect upon him—he had not even once recalled it. But now it seemed to him that that meeting had had in it something very important and poetic.

"Peter Kirílovich, come here! We have recognized you," he now seemed to hear the words she had uttered and to see before him her eyes, her smile, her traveling hood, and a stray lock of her hair... and there seemed to him something pathetic and touching in all this.

Having finished his tale about the enchanting Polish lady, the captain asked Pierre if he had ever experienced a similar impulse to sacrifice himself for love and a feeling of envy of the legitimate husband.

Challenged by this question Pierre raised his head and felt a need to express the thoughts that filled his mind. He began to explain that he understood love for a woman somewhat differently. He said that in all his life he had loved and still loved only one woman, and that she could never be his.

"Tiens!" said the captain.

Pierre then explained that he had loved this woman from his earliest years, but that he had not dared to think of her because she was too young, and because he had been an illegitimate son without a name. Afterwards when he had received a name and wealth he dared not think of her because he loved her too well, placing her far above everything in the world, and especially therefore above himself.

When he had reached this point, Pierre asked the captain whether he understood that.

The captain made a gesture signifying that even if he did not understand it he begged Pierre to continue.

"Platónic love, clouds..." he muttered.

Whether it was the wine he had drunk, or an impulse of frankness, or the thought that this man did not, and never would, know any of those who played a part in his story, or whether it was all these things together, something loosened Pierre's tongue. Speaking thickly and with a faraway look in his shining eyes, he told the whole story of his life: his marriage, Natásha's love for his best friend, her betrayal of him, and all his own simple relations with her. Urged on by Ramballe's questions he also told what he had at first concealed— his own position and even his name.

More than anything else in Pierre's story the captain was impressed by the fact that Pierre was very rich, had two mansions in Moscow, and that he had abandoned everything and not left the city, but remained there concealing his name and station.

When it was late at night they went out together into the street. The night was warm and light. To the left of the house on the Pokróvka a fire glowed—the first of those that were beginning in Moscow. To the right and high up in the sky was the sickle of the waning moon and opposite to it hung that bright comet which was connected in Pierre's heart with his love. At the gate stood Gerásim, the cook, and two Frenchmen. Their laughter and their mutually incomprehensible remarks in two languages could be heard. They were looking at the glow seen in the town.

There was nothing terrible in the one small, distant fire in the immense city.

Gazing at the high starry sky, at the moon, at the comet, and at the glow from the fire, Pierre experienced a joyful emotion. "There now, how good it is, what more does one need?" thought he. And suddenly remembering his intention he grew dizzy and felt so faint that he leaned against the fence to save himself from falling.

Without taking leave of his new friend, Pierre left the gate with unsteady steps and returning to his room lay down on the sofa and immediately fell asleep.

CHAPTER XXX

The glow of the first fire that began on the second of September was watched from the various roads by the fugitive Muscovites and by the retreating troops, with many different feelings.

The Rostóv party spent the night at Mytíshchi, fourteen miles from Moscow. They had started so late on the first of September, the road had been so blocked by vehicles and troops, so many things had been forgotten for which servants were sent back, that they had decided to spend that night at a place three miles out of Moscow. The next morning they woke late and were again delayed so often that they only got as far as Great Mytíshchi. At ten o'clock that evening the Rostóv family and the wounded traveling with them were all distributed in the yards and huts of that large village. The Rostóvs' servants and coachmen and the orderlies of the wounded officers, after attending to their masters, had supper, fed the horses, and came out into the porches.

In a neighboring hut lay Raévski's adjutant with a fractured wrist. The awful pain he suffered made him moan incessantly and piteously, and his moaning sounded terrible in the darkness of the autumn night. He had spent the first night in the same yard as the Rostóvs. The countess said she had been unable to close her eyes on account of his moaning, and at Mytíshchi she moved into a worse hut simply to be farther away from the wounded man.

In the darkness of the night one of the servants noticed, above the high body of a coach standing before the porch, the small glow of another fire. One glow had long been visible and everybody knew that it was Little Mytíshchi burning—set on fire by Mamónov's Cossacks.

"But look here, brothers, there's another fire!" remarked an orderly.

All turned their attention to the glow.

"But they told us Little Mytíshchi had been set on fire by Mamónov's Cossacks."

"But that's not Mytíshchi, it's farther away."

"Look, it must be in Moscow!"

Two of the gazers went round to the other side of the coach and sat down on its steps.

"It's more to the left, why, Little Mytíshchi is over there, and this is right on the other side."

Several men joined the first two.

"See how it's flaring," said one. "That's a fire in Moscow: either in the Sushchévski or the Rogózhski quarter."

No one replied to this remark and for some time they all gazed silently at the spreading flames of the second fire in the distance.

Old Daniel Teréntich, the count's valet (as he was called), came up to the group and shouted at Míshka.

"What are you staring at, you good-for-nothing?... The count will be calling and there's nobody there; go and gather the clothes together."

"I only ran out to get some water," said Míshka.

"But what do you think, Daniel Teréntich? Doesn't it look as if that glow were in Moscow?" remarked one of the footmen.

Daniel Teréntich made no reply, and again for a long time they were all silent. The glow spread, rising and falling, farther and farther still.

"God have mercy.... It's windy and dry..." said another voice.

"Just look! See what it's doing now. O Lord! You can even see the crows flying. Lord have mercy on us sinners!"

"They'll put it out, no fear!"

"Who's to put it out?" Daniel Teréntich, who had hitherto been silent, was heard to say. His voice was calm and deliberate. "Moscow it is, brothers," said he. "Mother Moscow, the white..." his voice faltered, and he gave way to an old man's sob.

And it was as if they had all only waited for this to realize the significance for them of the glow they were watching. Sighs were heard, words of prayer, and the sobbing of the count's old valet.

CHAPTER XXXI

The valet, returning to the cottage, informed the count that Moscow was burning. The count donned his dressing gown and went out to look. Sónya and Madame Schoss, who had not yet undressed, went out with him. Only Natásha and the countess remained in the room. Pétya was no longer with the family, he had gone on with his regiment which was making for Tróitsa.

The countess, on hearing that Moscow was on fire, began to cry. Natásha, pale, with a fixed look, was sitting on the bench under the icons just where she had sat down on arriving and paid no attention to her father's words. She was listening to the ceaseless moaning of the adjutant, three houses off.

"Oh, how terrible," said Sónya returning from the yard chilled and frightened. "I believe the whole of Moscow will burn, there's an awful glow! Natásha, do look! You can see it from the window," she said to her cousin, evidently wishing to distract her mind.

But Natásha looked at her as if not understanding what was said to her and again fixed her eyes on the corner of the stove. She had been in this condition of stupor since the morning, when Sónya, to the surprise and annoyance of the countess, had for some unaccountable reason found it necessary to tell Natásha of Prince Andrew's wound and of his being with their party. The countess had seldom been so angry with anyone as she was with Sónya. Sónya had cried and begged to be forgiven and now, as if trying to atone for her fault, paid unceasing attention to her cousin.

"Look, Natásha, how dreadfully it is burning!" said she.

"What's burning?" asked Natásha. "Oh, yes, Moscow."

And as if in order not to offend Sónya and to get rid of her, she turned her face to the window, looked out in such a way that it was evident that she could not see anything, and again settled down in her former attitude.

"But you didn't see it!"

"Yes, really I did," Natásha replied in a voice that pleaded to be left in peace.

Both the countess and Sónya understood that, naturally, neither Moscow nor the burning of Moscow nor anything else could seem of importance to Natásha.

The count returned and lay down behind the partition. The countess went up to her daughter and touched her head with the back of her hand as she was wont to do when Natásha was ill, then touched her forehead with her lips as if to feel whether she was feverish, and finally kissed her.

"You are cold. You are trembling all over. You'd better lie down," said the countess.

"Lie down? All right, I will. I'll lie down at once," said Natásha.

When Natásha had been told that morning that Prince Andrew was seriously wounded and was traveling with their party, she had at first asked many questions: Where was he going? How was he wounded? Was it serious? And could she see him? But after she had been told that she could not see him, that he was seriously wounded but that his life was not in danger, she ceased to ask questions or to speak at all, evidently disbelieving what they told her, and convinced that say what she might she would still be told the same. All the way she had sat motionless in a corner of the coach with wide open eyes, and the expression in them which the countess knew so well and feared so much, and now she sat in the same way on the bench where she had seated herself on arriving. She was planning something and either deciding or had already decided something in her mind. The countess knew this, but what it might be she did not know, and this alarmed and tormented her.

"Natásha, undress, darling; lie down on my bed."

A bed had been made on a bedstead for the countess only. Madame Schoss and the two girls were to sleep on some hay on the floor.

"No, Mamma, I will lie down here on the floor," Natásha replied irritably and she went to the window and opened it. Through the open window the moans of the adjutant could be heard more distinctly. She put her head out into the damp night air, and the countess saw her slim neck shaking with sobs and throbbing against the window frame. Natásha knew it was not Prince Andrew who was moaning. She knew Prince Andrew was in the same yard as themselves and in a part of the hut across the passage; but this dreadful incessant moaning made her sob. The countess exchanged a look with Sónya.

"Lie down, darling; lie down, my pet," said the countess, softly touching Natásha's shoulders. "Come, lie down."

"Oh, yes... I'll lie down at once," said Natásha, and began hurriedly undressing, tugging at the tapes of her petticoat.

When she had thrown off her dress and put on a dressing jacket, she sat down with her foot under her on the bed that had been made up on the floor, jerked her thin and rather short plait of hair to the front, and began replaiting it. Her long, thin, practiced fingers rapidly unplaited, replaited, and tied up her plait. Her head moved from side to side from habit, but her eyes, feverishly wide, looked fixedly before her. When her toilet for the night was finished she sank gently onto the sheet spread over the hay on the side nearest the door.

"Natásha, you'd better lie in the middle," said Sónya.

"I'll stay here," muttered Natásha. "Do lie down," she added crossly, and buried her face in the pillow.

The countess, Madame Schoss, and Sónya undressed hastily and lay down. The small lamp in front of the icons was the only light left in the room. But in the yard there was a light from the fire at Little Mytíshchi a mile and a half away, and through the night came the noise of people shouting at a tavern Mamónov's Cossacks had set up across the street, and the adjutant's unceasing moans could still be heard.

For a long time Natásha listened attentively to the sounds that reached her from inside and outside the room and did not move. First she heard her mother praying and sighing and the creaking of her bed under her, then Madame Schoss' familiar whistling snore and Sónya'sgentle breathing. Then the countess called to Natásha. Natásha did not answer.

"I think she's asleep, Mamma," said Sónya softly.

After a short silence the countess spoke again but this time no one replied.

Soon after that Natásha heard her mother's even breathing. Natásha did not move, though her little bare foot, thrust out from under the quilt, was growing cold on the bare floor.

As if to celebrate a victory over everybody, a cricket chirped in a crack in the wall. A cock crowed far off and another replied near by. The shouting in the tavern had died down; only the moaning of the adjutant was heard. Natásha sat up.

"Sónya, are you asleep? Mamma?" she whispered.

No one replied. Natásha rose slowly and carefully, crossed herself, and stepped cautiously on the cold and dirty floor with her slim, supple, bare feet. The boards of the floor creaked. Stepping cautiously from one foot to the other she ran like a kitten the few steps to the door and grasped the cold door handle.

It seemed to her that something heavy was beating rhythmically against all the walls of the room: it was her own heart, sinking with alarm and terror and overflowing with love.

She opened the door and stepped across the threshold and onto the cold, damp earthen floor of the passage. The cold she felt refreshed her. With her bare feet she touched a sleeping man, stepped over him, and opened the door into the part of the hut where Prince Andrew lay. It was dark in there. In the farthest corner, on a bench beside a bed on which something was lying, stood a tallow candle with a long, thick, and smoldering wick.

From the moment she had been told that morning of Prince Andrew's wound and his presence there, Natásha had resolved to see him. She did not know why she had to, she knew the meeting would be painful, but felt the more convinced that it was necessary.

All day she had lived only in hope of seeing him that night. But now that the moment had come she was filled with dread of what she might see. How was he maimed? What was left of him? Was he like that incessant moaning of the adjutant's? Yes, he was altogether like that. In her imagination he was that terrible moaning personified. When she saw an indistinct shape in the corner, and mistook his knees raised under the quilt for his shoulders, she imagined a horrible body there, and stood still in terror. But an irresistible impulse drew her forward. She cautiously took one step and then another, and found herself in the middle of a small room containing baggage. Another man—Timókhin—was lying in a corner on the benches beneath the icons, and two others—the doctor and a valet—lay on the floor.

The valet sat up and whispered something. Timókhin, kept awake by the pain in his wounded leg, gazed with wide-open eyes at this strange apparition of a girl in a white chemise, dressing jacket, and nightcap. The valet's sleepy, frightened exclamation, "What do you want? What's the matter?" made Natásha approach more swiftly to what was lying in the corner. Horribly unlike a man as that body looked, she must see him. She passed the valet, the snuff fell from the candle wick, and she saw Prince Andrew clearly with his arms outside the quilt, and such as she had always seen him.

He was the same as ever, but the feverish color of his face, his glittering eyes rapturously turned toward her, and especially his neck, delicate as a child's, revealed by the turn-down collar of his shirt, gave him a peculiarly innocent, childlike look, such as she had never seen on him before. She went up to him and with a swift, flexible, youthful movement dropped on her knees.

He smiled and held out his hand to her.

CHAPTER XXXII

Seven days had passed since Prince Andrew found himself in the ambulance station on the field of Borodinó. His feverish state and the inflammation of his bowels, which were injured, were in the doctor's opinion sure to carry him off. But on the seventh day he ate with pleasure a piece of bread with some tea, and the doctor noticed that his temperature was lower. He had regained consciousness that morning. The first night after they left Moscow had been fairly warm and he had remained in the *calèche*, but at Mytíshchi the wounded man himself asked to be taken out and given some tea. The pain caused by his removal into the hut had made him groan aloud and again lose consciousness. When he had been placed on his camp bed he lay for a long time motionless with closed eyes. Then he opened them and whispered softly: "And the tea?" His remembering such a small detail of everyday life astonished the doctor. He felt Prince Andrew's pulse, and to his surprise and dissatisfaction found it had improved. He was dissatisfied because he knew by experience that if his patient did not die now, he would do so a little later with greater suffering. Timókhin, the red-nosed major of Prince Andrew's regiment, had joined him in Moscow and was being taken along with him, having been wounded in the leg at the battle of Borodinó. They were accompanied by a doctor, Prince Andrew's valet, his coachman, and two orderlies.

They gave Prince Andrew some tea. He drank it eagerly, looking with feverish eyes at the door in front of him as if trying to understand and remember something.

"I don't want any more. Is Timókhin here?" he asked.

Timókhin crept along the bench to him.

"I am here, your excellency."

"How's your wound?"

"Mine, sir? All right. But how about you?"

Prince Andrew again pondered as if trying to remember something.

"Couldn't one get a book?" he asked.

"What book?"

"The Gospels. I haven't one."

The doctor promised to procure it for him and began to ask how he was feeling. Prince Andrew answered all his questions reluctantly but reasonably, and then said he wanted a bolster placed under him as he was uncomfortable and in great pain. The doctor and valet lifted the cloak with which he was covered and, making wry faces at the noisome smell of mortifying flesh that came from the wound, began examining that dreadful place. The doctor was very much displeased about something and made a change in the dressings, turning the wounded man over so that he groaned again and grew unconscious and delirious from the agony. He kept asking them to get him the book and put it under him.

"What trouble would it be to you?" he said. "I have not got one. Please get it for me and put it under for a moment," he pleaded in a piteous voice.

The doctor went into the passage to wash his hands.

"You fellows have no conscience," said he to the valet who was pouring water over his hands. "For just one moment I didn't look after you... It's such pain, you know, that I wonder how he can bear it."

"By the Lord Jesus Christ, I thought we had put something under him!" said the valet.

The first time Prince Andrew understood where he was and what was the matter with him and remembered being wounded and how was when he asked to be carried into the hut after his *calèche* had stopped at Mytíshchi. After growing confused from pain while being carried into the hut he again regained consciousness, and while drinking tea once more recalled all that had happened to him, and above all vividly remembered the moment at the ambulance station when, at the sight of the sufferings of a man he disliked, those new thoughts had come to him which promised him happiness. And those thoughts, though now vague and indefinite, again possessed his soul. He remembered that he had now a new source of happiness and that this happiness had something to do with the Gospels. That was why he asked for a copy of them. The uncomfortable position in which they had put him and turned him over again confused his thoughts, and when he came to himself a third time it was in the complete stillness of the night. Everybody near him was sleeping. A cricket chirped from across the passage; someone was shouting and singing in the street; cockroaches rustled on the table, on the icons, and on the walls, and a big fly flopped at the head of the bed and around the candle beside him, the wick of which was charred and had shaped itself like a mushroom.

His mind was not in a normal state. A healthy man usually thinks of, feels, and remembers innumerable things simultaneously, but has the power and will to select one sequence of thoughts or events on which to fix his whole attention. A healthy man can tear himself away from the deepest reflections to say a civil word to someone who comes in and can then return again to his own thoughts. But Prince Andrew's mind was not in a normal state in that respect. All the powers of his mind were more active and clearer than ever, but they acted apart from his will. Most diverse thoughts and images occupied him simultaneously. At times his brain suddenly began to work with a vigor, clearness, and depth it had never reached when he was in health, but suddenly in the midst of its work it would turn to some unexpected idea and he had not the strength to turn it back again.

"Yes, a new happiness was revealed to me of which man cannot be deprived," he thought as he lay in the semidarkness of the quiet hut, gazing fixedly before him with feverish wide open eyes. "A happiness lying beyond material forces, outside the material influences that act on man—a happiness of the soul alone, the happiness of loving. Every man can understand it, but to conceive it and enjoin it was possible only for God. But how did God enjoin that law? And why was the Son...?"

And suddenly the sequence of these thoughts broke off, and Prince Andrew heard (without knowing whether it was a delusion or reality) a soft whispering voice incessantly and rhythmically repeating "piti-piti-piti," and then "titi," and then again "piti-piti-piti," and "ti-ti" once more. At the same time he felt that above his face, above the very middle of it, some strange airy structure was being erected out of slender needles or splinters, to the sound of this whispered music. He felt that he had to balance carefully (though it was difficult) so that this airy structure should not collapse; but nevertheless it kept collapsing and again slowly rising to the sound of whispered rhythmic music—"it stretches, stretches, spreading out and stretching," said Prince Andrew to himself. While listening to this whispering and feeling the sensation of this drawing out and the construction of this edifice of needles, he also saw by glimpses a red halo round the candle, and heard the rustle of the cockroaches and the buzzing of the fly that flopped against his pillow and his face. Each time the fly touched his face it gave him a burning sensation and yet to his surprise it did not destroy the structure, though it knocked against the very region of his face where it was rising. But besides this there was something else of importance. It was something white by the door—the statue of a sphinx, which also oppressed him.

"But perhaps that's my shirt on the table," he thought, "and that's my legs, and that is the door, but why is it always stretching and drawing itself out, and 'piti-piti-piti' and 'ti-ti' and 'piti-piti-piti'...? That's enough, please leave off!" Prince Andrew painfully entreated someone. And suddenly thoughts and feelings again swam to the surface of his mind with peculiar clearness and force.

"Yes—love," he thought again quite clearly. "But not love which loves for something, for some quality, for some purpose, or for some reason, but the love which I—while dying—first experienced when I saw my enemy and yet loved him. I experienced that feeling of love which is the very essence of the soul and does not require an object. Now again I feel that bliss. To love one's neighbors, to love one's enemies, to love everything, to love God in all His manifestations.

It is possible to love someone dear to you with human love, but an enemy can only be loved by divine love. That is why I experienced such joy when I felt that I loved that man. What has become of him? Is he alive?...

"When loving with human love one may pass from love to hatred, but divine love cannot change. No, neither death nor anything else can destroy it. It is the very essence of the soul. Yet how many people have I hated in my life? And of them all, I loved and hated none as I did her." And he vividly pictured to himself Natásha, not as he had done in the past with nothing but her charms which gave him delight, but for the first time picturing to himself her soul. And he understood her feelings, her sufferings, shame, and remorse. He now understood for the first time all the cruelty of his rejection of her, the cruelty of his rupture with her. "If only it were possible for me to see her once more! Just once, looking into those eyes to say..."

"Piti-piti-piti and ti-ti and piti-piti-piti boom!" flopped the fly.... And his attention was suddenly carried into another world, a world of reality and delirium in which something particular was happening. In that world some structure was still being erected and did not fall, something was still stretching out, and the candle with its red halo was still burning, and the same shirtlike sphinx lay near the door; but besides all this something creaked, there was a whiff of fresh air, and a new white sphinx appeared, standing at the door. And that sphinx had the pale face and shining eyes of the very Natásha of whom he had just been thinking.

"Oh, how oppressive this continual delirium is," thought Prince Andrew, trying to drive that face from his imagination. But the face remained before him with the force of reality and drew nearer. Prince Andrew wished to return to that former world of pure thought, but he could not, and delirium drew him back into its domain. The soft whispering voice continued its rhythmic murmur, something oppressed him and stretched out, and the strange face was before him. Prince Andrew collected all his strength in an effort to recover his senses, he moved a little, and suddenly there was a ringing in his ears, a dimness in his eyes, and like a man plunged into water he lost consciousness. When he came to himself, Natásha, that same living Natásha whom of all people he most longed to love with this new pure divine love that had been revealed to him, was kneeling before him. He realized that it was the real living Natásha, and he was not surprised but quietly happy. Natásha, motionless on her knees (she was unable to stir), with frightened eyes riveted on him, was restraining her sobs. Her face was pale and rigid. Only in the lower part of it something quivered.

Prince Andrew sighed with relief, smiled, and held out his hand.

"You?" he said. "How fortunate!"

With a rapid but careful movement Natásha drew nearer to him on her knees and, taking his hand carefully, bent her face over it and began kissing it, just touching it lightly with her lips.

"Forgive me!" she whispered, raising her head and glancing at him. "Forgive me!"

"I love you," said Prince Andrew.

"Forgive...!"

"Forgive what?" he asked.

"Forgive me for what I ha-ve do-ne!" faltered Natásha in a scarcely audible, broken whisper, and began kissing his hand more rapidly, just touching it with her lips.

"I love you more, better than before," said Prince Andrew, lifting her face with his hand so as to look into her eyes.

Those eyes, filled with happy tears, gazed at him timidly, compassionately, and with joyous love. Natásha's thin pale face, with its swollen lips, was more than plain—it was dreadful. But Prince Andrew did not see that, he saw her shining eyes which were beautiful. They heard the sound of voices behind them.

Peter the valet, who was now wide awake, had roused the doctor. Timókhin, who had not slept at all because of the pain in his leg, had long been watching all that was going on, carefully covering his bare body with the sheet as he huddled up on his bench.

"What's this?" said the doctor, rising from his bed. "Please go away, madam!"

At that moment a maid sent by the countess, who had noticed her daughter's absence, knocked at the door.

Like a somnambulist aroused from her sleep Natásha went out of the room and, returning to her hut, fell sobbing on her bed.

From that time, during all the rest of the Rostóvs' journey, at every halting place and wherever they spent a night, Natásha never left the wounded Bolkónski, and the doctor had to admit that he had not expected from a young girl either such firmness or such skill in nursing a wounded man.

Dreadful as the countess imagined it would be should Prince Andrew die in her daughter's arms during the journey—as, judging by what the doctor said, it seemed might easily happen—she could not oppose Natásha. Though with the intimacy now established between the wounded man and Natásha the thought occurred that should he recover their former engagement would be renewed, no one— least of all Natásha and Prince Andrew—spoke of this: the unsettled question of life and death, which hung not only over Bolkónski but over all Russia, shut out all other considerations.

CHAPTER XXXIII

On the third of September Pierre awoke late. His head was aching, the clothes in which he had slept without undressing felt uncomfortable on his body, and his mind had a dim consciousness of something shameful he had done the day before. That something shameful was his yesterday's conversation with Captain Ramballe.

It was eleven by the clock, but it seemed peculiarly dark out of doors. Pierre rose, rubbed his eyes, and seeing the pistol with an engraved stock which Gerásim had replaced on the writing table, he remembered where he was and what lay before him that very day.

"Am I not too late?" he thought. "No, probably *he* won't make his entry into Moscow before noon."

Pierre did not allow himself to reflect on what lay before him, but hastened to act.

After arranging his clothes, he took the pistol and was about to go out. But it then occurred to him for the first time that he certainly could not carry the weapon in his hand through the streets. It was difficult to hide such a big pistol even under his wide coat. He could not carry it unnoticed in his belt or under his arm. Besides, it had been discharged, and he had not had time to reload it. "No matter, the dagger will do," he said to himself, though when planning his design he had more than once come to the conclusion that the chief mistake made by the student in 1809 had been to try to kill Napoleon with a dagger. But as his chief aim consisted not in carrying out his design, but in proving to himself that he would not abandon his intention and was doing all he could to achieve it, Pierre hastily took the blunt jagged dagger in a green sheath which he had bought at the Súkharev market with the pistol, and hid it under his waistcoat.

Having tied a girdle over his coat and pulled his cap low on his head, Pierre went down the corridor, trying to avoid making a noise or meeting the captain, and passed out into the street.

The conflagration, at which he had looked with so much indifference the evening before, had greatly increased during the night. Moscow was on fire in several places. The buildings in Carriage Row, across the river, in the Bazaar and the Povarskóy, as well as the barges on the Moskvá River and the timber yards by the Dorogomílov Bridge, were all ablaze.

Pierre's way led through side streets to the Povarskóy and from there to the church of St. Nicholas on the Arbát, where he had long before decided that the deed should be done. The gates of most of the houses were locked and the shutters up. The streets and lanes were deserted. The air was full of smoke and the smell of burning. Now and then he met Russians with anxious and timid faces, and Frenchmen with an air not of the city but of the camp, walking in the middle of the streets. Both the Russians and the French looked at Pierre with surprise. Besides his height and stoutness, and the strange morose look of suffering in his face and whole figure, the Russians stared at Pierre because they could not make out to what class he could belong. The French followed him with astonishment in their eyes chiefly because Pierre, unlike all the other Russians who gazed at the French with fear and curiosity, paid no attention to them. At the gate of one house three Frenchmen, who were explaining something to some Russians who did not understand them, stopped Pierre asking if he did not know French.

Pierre shook his head and went on. In another side street a sentinel standing beside a green caisson shouted at him, but only when the shout was threateningly repeated and he heard the click of the man's musket as he raised it did Pierre understand that he had to pass on the other side of the street. He heard nothing and saw nothing of what went on around him. He carried his resolution within himself in terror and haste, like something dreadful and alien to him, for, after the previous night's experience, he was afraid of losing it. But he was not destined to bring his mood safely to his destination. And even had he not been hindered by anything on the way, his intention could not now have been carried out, for Napoleon had passed the Arbát more than four hours previously on his way from the Dorogomílov suburb to the Krémlin, and was now sitting in a very gloomy frame of mind in a royal study in the Krémlin, giving detailed and exact orders as to measures to be taken immediately to extinguish the fire, to prevent looting, and to reassure the inhabitants. But Pierre did not know this; he was entirely absorbed in what lay before him, and was tortured—as those are who obstinately undertake a task that is impossible for them not because of its difficulty but because of its incompatibility with their natures—by the fear of weakening at the decisive moment and so losing his self-esteem.

Though he heard and saw nothing around him he found his way by instinct and did not go wrong in the side streets that led to the Povarskóy.

As Pierre approached that street the smoke became denser and denser—he even felt the heat of the fire. Occasionally curly tongues of flame rose from under the roofs of the houses. He met more people in the streets and they were more excited. But Pierre, though he felt that something unusual was happening around him, did not realize that he was approaching the fire. As he was going along a footpath across a wide-open space adjoining the Povarskóy on one side and the gardens of Prince Gruzínski's house on the other, Pierre suddenly heard the desperate weeping of a woman close to him. He stopped as if awakening from a dream and lifted his head.

By the side of the path, on the dusty dry grass, all sorts of household goods lay in a heap: featherbeds, a samovar, icons, and trunks. On the ground, beside the trunks, sat a thin woman no longer young, with long, prominent upper teeth, and wearing a black cloak and cap. This woman, swaying to and fro and muttering something, was choking with sobs. Two girls of about ten and twelve, dressed in dirty short frocks and cloaks, were staring at their mother with a look of stupefaction on their pale frightened faces. The youngest child, a boy of about seven, who wore an overcoat and an immense cap evidently not his own, was crying in his old nurse's arms. A dirty, barefooted maid was sitting on a trunk, and, having undone her pale-colored plait, was pulling it straight and sniffing at her singed hair. The woman's husband, a short, round-shouldered man in the undress uniform of a civilian official, with sausage-shaped whiskers and showing under his square-set cap the hair smoothly brushed forward over his temples, with expressionless face was moving the trunks, which were placed one on another, and was dragging some garments from under them.

As soon as she saw Pierre, the woman almost threw herself at his feet.

"Dear people, good Christians, save me, help me, dear friends... help us, somebody," she muttered between her sobs. "My girl... My daughter! My youngest daughter is left behind. She's burned! Ooh! Was it for this I nursed you.... Ooh!"

"Don't, Mary Nikoláevna!" said her husband to her in a low voice, evidently only to justify himself before the stranger. "Sister must have taken her, or else where can she be?" he added.

"Monster! Villain!" shouted the woman angrily, suddenly ceasing to weep. "You have no heart, you don't feel for your own child! Another man would have rescued her from the fire. But this is a monster and neither a man nor a father! You, honored sir, are a noble man," she went on, addressing Pierre rapidly between her sobs. "The fire broke out alongside, and blew our way, the maid called out 'Fire!' and we rushed to collect our things. We ran out just as we were.... This is what we have brought away.... The icons, and my dowry bed, all the rest is lost. We seized the children. But not Katie! Ooh! O Lord!..." and again she began to sob. "My child, my dear one! Burned, burned!"

"But where was she left?" asked Pierre.

From the expression of his animated face the woman saw that this man might help her.

"Oh, dear sir!" she cried, seizing him by the legs. "My benefactor, set my heart at ease.... Aníska, go, you horrid girl, show him the way!" she cried to the maid, angrily opening her mouth and still farther exposing her long teeth.

"Show me the way, show me, I... I'll do it," gasped Pierre rapidly.

The dirty maidservant stepped from behind the trunk, put up her plait, sighed, and went on her short, bare feet along the path. Pierre felt as if he had come back to life after a heavy swoon. He held his head higher, his eyes shone with the light of life, and with swift steps he followed the maid, overtook her, and came out on the Povarskóy. The whole street was full of clouds of black smoke. Tongues of flame here and there broke through that cloud. A great number of people crowded in front of the conflagration. In the middle of the street stood a French general saying something to those around him.

Pierre, accompanied by the maid, was advancing to the spot where the general stood, but the French soldiers stopped him.

"*On ne passe pas!*"* cried a voice.

* "You can't pass!"

"This way, uncle," cried the girl. "We'll pass through the side street, by the Nikúlins'!"

Pierre turned back, giving a spring now and then to keep up with her. She ran across the street, turned down a side street to the left, and, passing three houses, turned into a yard on the right.

"It's here, close by," said she and, running across the yard, opened a gate in a wooden fence and, stopping, pointed out to him a small wooden wing of the house, which was burning brightly and fiercely. One of its sides had fallen in, another was on fire, and bright flames issued from the openings of the windows and from under the roof.

As Pierre passed through the fence gate, he was enveloped by hot air and involuntarily stopped.

"Which is it? Which is your house?" he asked.

"Ooh!" wailed the girl, pointing to the wing. "That's it, that was our lodging. You've burned to death, our treasure, Katie, my precious little missy! Ooh!" lamented Aníska, who at the sight of the fire felt that she too must give expression to her feelings.

Pierre rushed to the wing, but the heat was so great that he involuntarily passed round in a curve and came upon the large house that was as yet burning only at one end, just below the roof, and around which swarmed a crowd of Frenchmen. At first Pierre did not realize what these men, who were dragging something out, were about; but seeing before him a Frenchman hitting a peasant with a blunt saber and trying to take from him a fox-fur coat, he vaguely understood that looting was going on there, but he had no time to dwell on that idea.

The sounds of crackling and the din of falling walls and ceilings, the whistle and hiss of the flames, the excited shouts of the people, and the sight of the swaying smoke, now gathering into thick black clouds and now soaring up with glittering sparks, with here and there dense sheaves of flame (now red and now like golden fish scales creeping along the walls), and the heat and smoke and rapidity of motion, produced on Pierre the usual animating effects of a conflagration. It had a peculiarly strong effect on him because at the sight of the fire he felt himself suddenly freed from the ideas that had weighed him down. He felt young, bright, adroit, and resolute. He ran round to the other side of the lodge and was about to dash into that part of it which was still standing, when just above his head he heard several voices shouting and then a cracking sound and the ring of something heavy falling close beside him.

Pierre looked up and saw at a window of the large house some Frenchmen who had just thrown out the drawer of a chest, filled with metal articles. Other French soldiers standing below went up to the drawer.

"What does this fellow want?" shouted one of them referring to Pierre.

"There's a child in that house. Haven't you seen a child?" cried Pierre.

"What's he talking about? Get along!" said several voices, and one of the soldiers, evidently afraid that Pierre might want to take from them some of the plate and bronzes that were in the drawer, moved threateningly toward him.

"A child?" shouted a Frenchman from above. "I did hear something squealing in the garden. Perhaps it's his brat that the fellow is looking for. After all, one must be human, you know...."

"Where is it? Where?" said Pierre.

"There! There!" shouted the Frenchman at the window, pointing to the garden at the back of the house. "Wait a bit—I'm coming down."

And a minute or two later the Frenchman, a black-eyed fellow with a spot on his cheek, in shirt sleeves, really did jump out of a window on the ground floor, and clapping Pierre on the shoulder ran with him into the garden.

"Hurry up, you others!" he called out to his comrades. "It's getting hot."

When they reached a gravel path behind the house the Frenchman pulled Pierre by the arm and pointed to a round, graveled space where a three-year-old girl in a pink dress was lying under a seat.

"There is your child! Oh, a girl, so much the better!" said the Frenchman. "Good-by, Fatty. We must be human, we are all mortal you know!" and the Frenchman with the spot on his cheek ran back to his comrades.

Breathless with joy, Pierre ran to the little girl and was going to take her in his arms. But seeing a stranger the sickly, scrofulous-looking child, unattractively like her mother, began to yell and run away. Pierre, however, seized her and lifted her in his arms. She screamed desperately and angrily and tried with her little hands to pull Pierre's hands away and to bite them with her slobbering mouth. Pierre was seized by a sense of horror and repulsion such as he had experienced when touching some nasty little animal. But he made an effort not to throw the child down and ran with her to the large house. It was now, however, impossible to get back the way he had come; the maid, Aníska, was no longer there, and Pierre with a feeling of pity and disgust pressed the wet, painfully sobbing child to himself as tenderly as he could and ran with her through the garden seeking another way out.

CHAPTER XXXIV

Having run through different yards and side streets, Pierre got back with his little burden to the Gruzínski garden at the corner of the Povarskóy. He did not at first recognize the place from which he had set out to look for the child, so crowded was it now with people and goods that had been dragged out of the houses. Besides Russian families who had taken refuge here from the fire with their belongings, there were several French soldiers in a variety of clothing. Pierre took no notice of them. He hurried to find the family of that civil servant in order to restore the daughter to her mother and go to save someone else. Pierre felt that he had still much to do and to do quickly. Glowing with the heat and from running, he felt at that moment more strongly than ever the sense of youth, animation, and determination that had come on him when he ran to save the child. She had now become quiet and, clinging with her little hands to Pierre's coat, sat on his arm gazing about her like some little wild animal. He glanced at her occasionally with a slight smile. He fancied he saw something pathetically innocent in that frightened, sickly little face.

He did not find the civil servant or his wife where he had left them. He walked among the crowd with rapid steps, scanning the various faces he met. Involuntarily he noticed a Georgian or Armenian family consisting of a very handsome old man of Oriental type, wearing a new, cloth-covered, sheepskin coat and new boots, an old woman of similar type, and a young woman. That very young woman seemed to Pierre the perfection of Oriental beauty, with her sharply outlined, arched, black eyebrows and the extraordinarily soft, bright color of her long, beautiful, expressionless face. Amid the scattered property and the crowd on the open space, she, in her rich satin cloak with a bright lilac shawl on her head, suggested a delicate exotic plant thrown out onto the snow. She was sitting on some bundles a little behind the old woman, and looked from under her long lashes with motionless, large, almond-shaped eyes at the ground before her. Evidently she was aware of her beauty and fearful because of it. Her face struck Pierre and, hurrying along by the fence, he turned several times to look at her. When he had reached the fence, still without finding those he sought, he stopped and looked about him.

With the child in his arms his figure was now more conspicuous than before, and a group of Russians, both men and women, gathered about him.

"Have you lost anyone, my dear fellow? You're of the gentry yourself, aren't you? Whose child is it?" they asked him.

Pierre replied that the child belonged to a woman in a black coat who had been sitting there with her other children, and he asked whether anyone knew where she had gone.

"Why, that must be the Anférovs," said an old deacon, addressing a pockmarked peasant woman. "Lord have mercy, Lord have mercy!" he added in his customary bass.

"The Anférovs? No," said the woman. "They left in the morning. That must be either Mary Nikoláevna's or the Ivánovs'!"

"He says 'a woman,' and Mary Nikoláevna is a lady," remarked a house serf.

"Do you know her? She's thin, with long teeth," said Pierre.

"That's Mary Nikoláevna! They went inside the garden when these wolves swooped down," said the woman, pointing to the French soldiers.

"O Lord, have mercy!" added the deacon.

"Go over that way, they're there. It's she! She kept on lamenting and crying," continued the woman. "It's she. Here, this way!"

But Pierre was not listening to the woman. He had for some seconds been intently watching what was going on a few steps away. He was looking at the Armenian family and at two French soldiers who had gone up to them. One of these, a nimble little man, was wearing a blue coat tied round the waist with a rope. He had a nightcap on his head and his feet were bare. The other, whose appearance particularly struck Pierre, was a long, lank, round-shouldered, fair-haired man, slow in his movements and with an idiotic expression of face. He wore a woman's loose gown of frieze, blue trousers, and large torn Hessian boots. The little barefooted Frenchman in the blue coat went up to the Armenians and, saying something, immediately seized the old man by his legs and the old man at once began pulling off his boots. The other in the frieze gown stopped in front of the beautiful Armenian girl and with his hands in his pockets stood staring at her, motionless and silent.

"Here, take the child!" said Pierre peremptorily and hurriedly to the woman, handing the little girl to her. "Give her back to them, give her back!" he almost shouted, putting the child, who began screaming, on the ground, and again looking at the Frenchman and the Armenian family.

The old man was already sitting barefoot. The little Frenchman had secured his second boot and was slapping one boot against the other. The old man was saying something in a voice broken by sobs, but Pierre caught but a glimpse of this, his whole attention was directed to the Frenchman in the frieze gown who meanwhile, swaying slowly from side to side, had drawn nearer to the young woman and taking his hands from his pockets had seized her by the neck.

The beautiful Armenian still sat motionless and in the same attitude, with her long lashes drooping as if she did not see or feel what the soldier was doing to her.

While Pierre was running the few steps that separated him from the Frenchman, the tall marauder in the frieze gown was already tearing from her neck the necklace the young Armenian was wearing, and the young woman, clutching at her neck, screamed piercingly.

"Let that woman alone!" exclaimed Pierre hoarsely in a furious voice, seizing the soldier by his round shoulders and throwing him aside.

The soldier fell, got up, and ran away. But his comrade, throwing down the boots and drawing his sword, moved threateningly toward Pierre.

"Voyons, pas de bêtises!" * he cried.

* "Look here, no nonsense!"

Pierre was in such a transport of rage that he remembered nothing and his strength increased tenfold. He rushed at the barefooted Frenchman and, before the latter had time to draw his sword, knocked him off his feet and hammered him with his fists. Shouts of approval were heard from the crowd around, and at the same moment a mounted patrol of French Uhlans appeared from round the corner. The Uhlans came up at a trot to Pierre and the Frenchman and surrounded them. Pierre remembered nothing of what happened after that. He only remembered beating someone and being beaten and finally feeling that his hands were bound and that a crowd of French soldiers stood around him and were searching him.

"Lieutenant, he has a dagger," were the first words Pierre understood.

"Ah, a weapon?" said the officer and turned to the barefooted soldier who had been arrested with Pierre. "All right, you can tell all about it at the court-martial." Then he turned to Pierre. "Do you speak French?"

Pierre looked around him with bloodshot eyes and did not reply. His face probably looked very terrible, for the officer said something in a whisper and four more Uhlans left the ranks and placed themselves on both sides of Pierre.

"Do you speak French?" the officer asked again, keeping at a distance from Pierre. "Call the interpreter."

A little man in Russian civilian clothes rode out from the ranks, and by his clothes and manner of speaking Pierre at once knew him to be a French salesman from one of the Moscow shops.

"He does not look like a common man," said the interpreter, after a searching look at Pierre.

"Ah, he looks very much like an incendiary," remarked the officer. "And ask him who he is," he added.

"Who are you?" asked the interpreter in poor Russian. "You must answer the chief."

"I will not tell you who I am. I am your prisoner—take me!" Pierre suddenly replied in French.

"Ah, ah!" muttered the officer with a frown. "Well then, march!"

A crowd had collected round the Uhlans. Nearest to Pierre stood the pockmarked peasant woman with the little girl, and when the patrol started she moved forward.

"Where are they taking you to, you poor dear?" said she. "And the little girl, the little girl, what am I to do with her if she's not theirs?" said the woman.

"What does that woman want?" asked the officer.

Pierre was as if intoxicated. His elation increased at the sight of the little girl he had saved.

"What does she want?" he murmured. "She is bringing me my daughter whom I have just saved from the flames," said he. "Good-by!" And without knowing how this aimless lie had escaped him, he went along with resolute and triumphant steps between the French soldiers.

The French patrol was one of those sent out through the various streets of Moscow by Durosnel's order to put a stop to the pillage, and especially to catch the incendiaries who, according to the general opinion which had that day originated among the higher French officers, were the cause of the conflagrations. After marching through a number of streets the patrol arrested five more Russian suspects: a small shopkeeper, two seminary students, a peasant, and a house serf, besides several looters. But of all these various suspected characters, Pierre was considered to be the most suspicious of all. When they had all been brought for the night to a large house on the Zúbov Rampart that was being used as a guardhouse, Pierre was placed apart under strict guard.